SAND CASTLES

SAND CASTLES

NANCY GOTTER GATES

FIVE STAR
A part of Gale, Cengage Learning

GALE
CENGAGE Learning

Detroit • New York • San Francisco • New Haven, Conn • Waterville, Maine • London

GALE
CENGAGE Learning

LIBRARY OF CONGRESS CATALOGING-IN-PUBLICATION DATA

Gates, Nancy Gotter.
   Sand castles / Nancy Gotter Gates. — 1st ed.
     p. cm.
   ISBN-13: 978-1-59414-826-2 (alk. paper)
   ISBN-10: 1-59414-826-0 (alk. paper)
   1. Self-realization in women—Fiction. 2. Marriage—Fiction. 3. Older women—Fiction. 4. Sarasota (Fla.)—Fiction. I. Title.
PS3607.A7887S26 2009
813'.6—dc22   2009027514

First Edition. First Printing: November 2009.
Published in 2009 in conjunction with Tekno Books.

Printed in the United States of America
1 2 3 4 5 6 7 13 12 11 10 09

In memory of my grandmother,
Fairie Mae Bond Jennings

ONE

The edge of a stepping stone felt like a dull knife blade in Virginia McAllister's side. But when she struggled to sit up, an electric-shock-like pain began at her left knee, traveling first up then down her leg so excruciating it took her breath away. She lay back down helpless. Her husband, Leland, was down on one knee beside her, and he picked up her hand and held it in both of his.

"Don't move, Ginny. An ambulance will be here any minute."

He took off his suit jacket and laid it across her, tucking it around her shoulders. She tried to smile to reassure him, but her lips trembled so from the pain and fright that she knew it must have looked grotesque.

The ladder hung precariously at an angle on top of the holly bush under the dining room window. God, why did she have to be such a damn perfectionist anyway?

Brimming with energy that morning, Ginny had been cleaning house for Leland's retirement party, and nothing eluded her keen eye for dirt or disorder. While hanging the newly washed Bing and Grondahl Christmas plates back on the dining room wall, she noticed fingerprints on the window that overlooked the back yard.

How had she missed those? She'd always considered spotless windows a badge of excellence in her housekeeping and she washed them often. Leland teased her about wearing the glass out from polishing, but it was ingrained in her.

She remembered then that Leland had told her one of the screens had a tear in it, and last night when he'd been out shopping, he must have bought a new one. He probably smeared the glass when he replaced the torn screen.

She gathered up her Windex™ and paper towels and left them on the back stoop as she wrestled the step ladder out of the garage. She placed it under the window—the house was slightly higher on the back as the yard sloped gradually from front to rear—retrieved the cleaner and towels and climbed up the ladder until she could reach the top pane where the fingerprints shone iridescently in the afternoon sun. She was reminded of the plaque that Donald had brought home from kindergarten years ago with his hand print preserved forever in kiln-fired red clay. It was her Mother's Day present, and it still occupied a place of honor on her dresser.

She felt more and more prone to these nostalgic moments. She almost hated to rub the prints off, but she laughed at her sentimentality and squirted the pane with cleaner. Just as she leaned forward to wipe away the smear, one of the ladder's legs dipped into what must have been a rabbit hole, throwing her off balance. She could feel the ladder give way under her, saw the Windex and paper towels rolling off the top, and tried to grab the windowsill and holly bush next to her as she fell, her stomach a tight knot of fear.

Her fingers slipped from the sill, and the holly bush served only to make long painful scratches on her arms as she clutched at the branches. Her right knee struck the ground first, on the edge of a paving stone that was part of a path from the back porch to the driveway.

For a few seconds she felt nothing but the shock and surprise of the fall. Then she realized her right leg was bent under her in a strange fashion, and she was unable to move. Her knee began to swell before her eyes, growing like a cantaloupe in time-lapse photography, until she was afraid it would burst.

Now the pain was beginning to edge into her consciousness, and within minutes it was sending excruciating waves throughout her body, making her faint and nauseous. She'd never experienced anything like it. She had not so much as sprained an ankle before. The only thing that could approach this feeling was labor pains, but that was tolerable because her mind was on the outcome—the baby—instead of the agony. Now there was nothing to distract her except, perhaps, her fear.

Unable to move, she knew it would be an hour or more before Leland got home from the office. Maybe Carla Hoff next door was home. She knew the Foresters on the other side were both at work. There was nothing to do but scream and hope someone would hear her.

For the first time in her life, she felt utterly helpless and alone. Fear caused her stomach to clench in a convulsed knot, and her hands twitched uncontrollably no matter how hard she tried to stop them. It was as if she no longer had influence over her own body.

"Help! Somebody help me!" Her voice only bounced off the back of the house in a pathetic echo. The only reply was the chirping of the birds. She called again and again. But no one answered.

The phone began to ring in the house. It rang again and again as though mimicking her cries and taunting her with help just beyond her reach.

Why *hadn't* she carried the cordless phone with her? The thought had never entered her mind.

There was nothing to do but wait for Leland.

She couldn't sit much longer the way she was, propped on her right arm, trying to keep the weight off her right leg. The roll of paper towels had landed in the holly bush beside her. She reached for it and found it was just beyond her fingertips.

Ginny thrust her body slightly upward, felt a new piercing pain in her knee from the slight motion, but managed to dislodge the roll, and it fell to the ground beside her. She picked it up, then eased her body slowly down till she was lying on her side, her leg bent oddly in front of her, and her head cradled on the roll of towels.

Two

Leland would be sixty-two on Sunday, May 22nd, and his company, Dunedin Industrial Rubber Products, was encouraging early retirements. They had "sweetened the pot" as Leland liked to say, offering their employees a pension at age sixty-two that would be the equivalent of what they'd normally get at sixty-five. Trying to cut their ranks by attrition rather than laying off, Dunedin was in the throes of downsizing like companies everywhere.

Leland had insisted that nothing could have pleased him more. After nearly three decades of on-the-road selling, he'd been promoted into management and charged with developing new products at their home plant in Columbus, Ohio. But he felt little satisfaction in this role, particularly now that the company was in financial difficulty that forced spending restraints he considered counterproductive if not downright senseless.

They'd had many dinner-table discussions about it. She remembered one night last winter when Leland came home as discouraged as she'd ever seen him. His lean face was drawn and pallid, and his blue eyes lacked their usual sparkle. Even his hair which was dark with just a little gray on the sides looked somehow unkempt as if he had combed his fingers through it in frustration. It wasn't like him. He normally radiated energy and joie de vivre.

"You'll never believe what happened," he said.

"Try me."

"You know that fake-wood polyurethane casket I've been trying to get them to develop?"

"Sure."

"Well, yesterday someone decided we had to see if our prototype would burn in case someone was cremated in one. We took it over to the crematorium, and the damn thing burned so well it caught the crematorium on fire. Didn't do much damage, but it sure shook them up."

Ginny could barely suppress her amusement, but for Leland's sake she kept a neutral expression. "Oh, so that's why you worked so late last night." She'd been asleep when he came in, and he'd hurried off that morning before she got up.

"Yeah, all hell broke loose as you can imagine. But the clincher came today. When I got back to the plant, someone had broken up the $50,000 mold. I knew we could fix the problem, but they didn't even want to try. Why make an effort to develop new products if they're only going to sabotage them?"

"Oh, Leland, that's a shame." She knew how frustrated he was by the MBAs and "bean counters" who knew nothing about the business he'd helped to build.

He often confided in Ginny that he didn't really care whether the company went down the tubes or not. He couldn't wait to get out of there. He stressed that he'd had enough foresight to invest wisely over the years, so if his pension should ever become imperiled, he would have other income.

But he couldn't fool her. After thirty-eight years of marriage, Ginny sensed what he would never admit out loud. Even though he'd had his differences with the company in recent years, like so many men, Leland's identity was tightly bound up with his job, and she was sure he had anxieties about being cut adrift. He'd never had many hobbies and interests outside of work except for gardening, and he couldn't do that during the long winter months. What was he going to do with himself? She'd heard stories from friends about restless husbands who were under foot all day making their lives miserable.

Ginny called her daughter-in-law Susan about the combination birthday/retirement party as soon as she decided to have it. Donald and his wife maintained such busy schedules they rarely came down from Cleveland to visit. She wanted to make sure they kept the day clear for Leland's special celebration.

Surprisingly, Susan answered on the second ring. She was seldom home in the evenings as she often worked late.

"Hi, Susan, it's Ginny." Susan had never called her Mom. "How are things with you two?"

"Busy, busy as always. In fact I was just about to dash off again to do some research on a couple of mergers we're working on."

Susan was an ambitious young lawyer who had every intention of being made a partner in record time.

There were many things Ginny admired about her daughter-in-law; she was brilliant and energetic, and she seemed to make Donald happy. Susan was always congenial but remote, unwilling to discuss anything personal, although Ginny had no intention of prying into their private life. When they were together, Susan could be effusive, but she talked mostly about work and clothes and material possessions, seemingly uninterested in anything Ginny had to say.

"I won't keep you. Just called to say I'm planning a surprise party for Leland to celebrate his birthday and retirement on Saturday, the 21st. I'm inviting everybody, the whole Washburn clan, the people at work, all the in-town friends. Pray for a nice day, because I don't know how we'll squeeze them all in the house."

"Sounds fabulous." Susan said. She tended to speak in

superlatives. "Donald's up to his eyeballs in the planning stages of the shopping center, but of course we'll be there."

Her words were gracious. Why did her tone sound so condescending? Ginny mentally kicked herself for being so super sensitive.

"I'm going to make it brunch so you kids can go back early if you need to." She knew Susan hated to be called a kid, but it came out automatically. Donald would always be their "kid," no matter what his age.

Donald was as ambitious as his wife. And Ginny thought she knew why. When he was fifteen, he ran away from home. It had been the typical scenario. His grades had been falling, his demeanor was sullen and secretive. One night when he and Leland had a shouting match over some chores he hadn't done, Donald stomped out the door and didn't come back.

Ginny and Leland were devastated and barely slept the next several nights. Leland took it personally, sure that he had somehow failed Donald. Ginny understood and shared Leland's angst; parents always feel they must accept blame no matter the circumstances. They shed many tears together. But she also felt peer pressure had a lot to do with it. However she couldn't convince Leland it wasn't all his fault.

A week later the sheriff picked up Donald walking along a rural road, and he was found to be carrying a small amount of marijuana. She and Leland sent him to a residential drug abuse program. It was successful, and Donald, unusually remorseful, had taken the path of overachiever ever since. Ginny often wondered if it was his method of atonement. She hoped he didn't kill himself trying to make up for a mistake made as an adolescent.

Having pinned down the most important guests, she called the rest of the family and friends and contacted the co-workers when Leland wasn't liable to overhear. She was pleased when almost everyone said they could come.

After the inviting had been done, she needed to decide on a menu. She dragged out all her cookbooks and read them front to back before making her selections. It was going to be glorious. She felt like a child anticipating Christmas.

She baked what she could ahead of time and froze it so that she would not be overwhelmed the morning of the party.

Ginny was sure Leland remained completely unaware of her preparations. He did none of the cooking so he never saw the packages that were accumulating in the freezer. And he was too preoccupied talking with the accountant and getting all his questions answered about his pension, medical coverage, and the other financial aspects of retirement to notice anything unusual going on at home.

On Monday of his final week of work, Ginny and Leland lingered over their coffee after supper.

"I've been thinking about our future," he said. "It seems to me we could have a lot more fun if we were somewhere warm during the winter months. I hadn't given it much thought until recently. I assumed we still had several years to decide. But since they sprang this retirement on me, it seems like we ought to get on with it and have a good time before our health goes, or we no longer have the energy."

"What do you mean when you say warm? The Cote d'Azure? The big island of Hawaii?" She got up and did an impromptu hula for him. She thought a trip to somewhere different every winter would be fun.

"You're crazy, you know it? Actually I was thinking about Florida. Year-round. The thing is you can golf and fish, too. There's not much fishing in Arizona, and California's too expensive." These two pastimes had always been part of Leland's retirement dreams.

A flicker of alarm went through Ginny. She hadn't realized

that he meant to *move* there! She had enjoyed their vacations in Florida, but she wasn't at all sure she wanted to be there permanently. "I don't know, Leland. I'd have to think about it some. Let's not be too hasty."

"Oh, well, of course we'd go down there and look around at condos and see what the situation's like. It's just a thought. Bob Mansfield told me today I should check out Sarasota. We haven't been there, and he says it's one of the nicest towns in the state."

"I'll go look at places any time you want. Let's just keep an open mind about it. I really don't know about being that far away from Donald and Susan."

"Wouldn't it be great," Leland smiled broadly as if he hadn't heard her, "if I never had to lift a snow shovel again? I don't want to have a heart attack like Andy Stein did last winter. Wouldn't you love to give away your boots and gloves to Goodwill? Just think, Ginny, I could play golf every day of the year!"

"And what would I be doing in the meantime?"

"Uh . . . well, I don't know," he looked at her in bewilderment, "the same things you always do, I guess, keep house and cook and read."

"But my friends are here in Columbus. And Donald and Susan are in Cleveland." Maybe they didn't come to Columbus that often, but she still didn't want to move hundreds of miles away from them.

"We never see the kids anyway. They're so involved in their own stuff. I'd bet we'd see more of them in Florida than we do here. They'd probably spend their vacations with us, particularly if we were near the water."

"You have a point," she had to admit.

"The same with your friends. I hear that if you live in Florida, you get covered up with company. And you can make new friends, too, after all."

"Well, we can think about it," she said to put an end to the discussion. She'd lived in this house for thirty-three years, and she wasn't ready to give it all up just like that.

Their conversation was very much on Ginny's mind the rest of the week as she cleaned the house thoroughly in anticipation of the party on Saturday. She washed and waxed the aging linoleum in the kitchen on her hands and knees till it glistened. She bought some appliance touch-up to cover the tiny nicks that she found on the edge of the sink and the refrigerator door. The room might be outdated but it would still look its best.

She left the living room and dining room till last because that was where most of the guests would gather, and she wanted it to be spotless. She pulled all the cushions out of the couch to vacuum it, glad that the bright design of flowers disguised the signs of wear. She dusted and swept and polished the tables till they gleamed.

She took a few minutes out to sit at the baby grand and play a simplified version of "Nadia's Theme," that was in an old *Sheet Music* magazine she'd had for years. She wasn't quite sure why she had subscribed to it. She played poorly and infrequently at that, but it gave her a reason to use the piano which had belonged to her grandfather and then her mother. When her father had died and her mother went into a nursing home, Ginny couldn't bear to sell it, and none of her brothers or sisters had a place for the old baby grand. Leland had paid to have it refinished—the old varnish had been crazed and chipped—and to have new ivory put on the yellowing keys. The sounding board had cracked from age so it could never be brought into absolute pitch. But she loved it and was rewarded with memories whenever she played.

It was after playing the piano that she'd washed the Christmas plates and discovered the fingerprints on the window. And her determination to have the house spotless for the party had changed her life forever.

THREE

The rest of that day would always be etched in Ginny's memory. Leland had come home early, thank God. It had been the next-to-last day of work for him, and there had been little to do except clean out his desk drawers. He became alarmed when there was no sign of Ginny or dinner. She'd always timed their evening meal to be ready the moment he came in the door. And she never went off without telling him.

He'd searched throughout the house, wondering if she was chatting with a neighbor and had forgotten the time. But that was so unlike her, he told her later, he dismissed that notion almost immediately.

He finally thought to look in the back yard, although, as he said, he couldn't imagine why she'd be there instead of cooking dinner. The gardening had always been his domain. She'd never had much interest in it, probably because as a teenager she'd been forced to work in her father's large garden when she wanted to be at the swimming pool. She never could understand anyone's love affair with gardening. Pulling weeds was such a bore. So after their marriage, the lines of demarcation were drawn: the house was hers, the yard his.

She vaguely remembered him telling her to be calm while he called for help. It hadn't been long before she heard sirens, and the police arrived, followed almost immediately by the emergency squad.

Even the severe pain and fear didn't prevent her from feeling embarrassed to be the center of so much attention. Now, after the futile attempts to get help when she fell, several neighbors appeared, attracted by the sirens. Myrna Caulfield from across the street was there, holding her hand and murmuring encouragement as the men worked over Ginny. Others stood by, obviously fascinated by her predicament. They meant well, but she wished they would leave.

Although the paramedics tried to be as gentle as possible, every move brought new waves of pain until she thought she could stand no more. The worst was when they had to straighten her leg in order to place an inflatable splint around it. She wept openly, no longer caring what people thought.

When they finally put her on a stretcher and placed her in the ambulance, she was relieved to be out of the circle of curious onlookers and at last on the way to a hospital where she hoped she could get something for the pain. It seemed to flow over her in waves that took her breath away. One of the men who had worked on her jumped in beside her and started an IV, to prevent shock she supposed. When they allowed Leland to climb in too, she felt he needed the IV more than she did. He looked so distraught she wanted to hold him in her arms and comfort him. Did all men fall apart like this in the face of medical emergencies?

Ginny finally was given some pain medication after a long exhausting session in the emergency room. The orthopedic surgeon examined her and they took X-rays before wheeling her into a room. The doctors put her leg in traction, saying they couldn't operate till the swelling had gone down, and after hours of being prodded and poked, she was finally left alone.

Well, not totally alone. Because there were no private rooms available, she had a roommate. Or at least she supposed there was someone behind the curtain pulled between the two beds. She was either asleep or did not want to talk.

"How are you feeling?" Ginny must have dozed off, and Leland's voice startled her. "I've been sitting in the waiting room for four hours and they finally let me come in." He stood over her in the dimly lit room.

"The pain's down to a dull roar since they gave me another shot." She took his hand in hers. "You must be exhausted, hon. Go on home and get yourself something to eat and go to bed. I'll be okay."

"Are you sure?"

"Look, I don't feel up to chatting. I'd just like to try to get some sleep, only I'm not sure I can manage it on my back like this. But I'll ask the nurse for a sleeping pill. You go on home."

"I'll come in first thing in the morning, then. Remember, they're having that retirement luncheon for me tomorrow, and I guess I've got to go to that." The company, cutting back as much as possible, no longer had elaborate retirement dinners, but had substituted less costly luncheons. Ginny was supposed to go and had bought a new dress for the occasion.

"Oh, no, I'd forgotten about that. I'm so sorry I spoiled it for you."

"I never really wanted to go in the first place. They make a lot of pompous speeches they don't really mean, and it's just a bunch of hypocritical hogwash as far as I'm concerned. But I'll go sit and smile dutifully for them anyway. No sense going out like a jerk. But, believe me, there was nothing to spoil."

"Heavens, Leland, I didn't know you felt that way about it."

"When I thought you were going too, I decided to keep my mouth shut so you'd be able to enjoy it. Now I'll just go and grin and bear it by myself. When you get out of this place, we'll celebrate with our own luncheon someplace special."

"You're a dear. Don't worry about me. I'll be okay."

"Good night. Have a good night's sleep." He kissed her on the forehead and left.

Saturday. Suddenly she remembered about the surprise party on Saturday, just two days away, about all the work she'd done baking things and cleaning the house. And she'd bought all kinds of ingredients for the last-minute cooking she'd planned. Maybe she could have it later on, or maybe they'd just have to eat it themselves. She couldn't even think about it tonight. She'd call her sister Melba in the morning and ask her to call everyone and explain what happened. Why did this accident have to happen at such an inopportune time?

FOUR

Ginny slept fitfully through the night, the pain rising to a crescendo as the shot wore off, then slowly receding again after another injection. She always slept on her right side, and it was very difficult to be forced to sleep on her back. When she finally dozed off, she began to dream about falling down a flight of stairs, which caused her to wake in alarm. After that she resisted sleep.

By morning she was glad to see the light filtering in from behind the drawn curtains. Pain always seems so much more intense at night because there's little to distract one from it. She hoped perhaps the sheer busyness and noise of the daytime routine would help take her mind off it.

"Hi." A soft voice roused her from half-sleep. At first she thought it was a nurse; then she realized it came from the other bed. The curtain between the beds had been pulled back, and a young woman, her frizzy blond hair framing her face, was smiling at her. Her left leg was in traction so that the two of them looked like mirror images, except that Ginny was probably close to forty years older than her roommate.

"I'm Joy Wentowski. We look like the Gimp Twins, don't we?"

"Ginny McAllister. Don't tell me you fell off a ladder, too."

"No, I managed to get in the way of some drunk who was on the wrong side of the road."

"I think they should lock those guys up and throw away the key."

"Me, too. Only this one managed to kill himself so at least he won't plow into anybody else."

Ginny shivered involuntarily. "What a terrible waste. Do you know how much longer you'll be in here?"

"The doctor said a couple of weeks. Sorry you had to get hurt, but it was sure getting lonesome in here."

Ginny glanced at Joy's left hand and noted she wore a wedding ring. Joy caught her look. "Dave, my husband, has to travel a lot on his job. He couldn't afford to take off to be with me so he's out selling in Wisconsin for two weeks. He won't be back till a week from Saturday."

"I'm married to a salesman, too, so I can sympathize. Leland spent a lot of time on the road over the years. But today's his last day of work, would you believe. They pretty much forced him to take early retirement. In fact, I'm missing the luncheon they're having for him. But at least he'll be home to help out when I get out of here."

"I'm not sure I'll have any help. My mom lives in Oregon and I've got a sister still at home, so Mom can't take off to come here. But I'll manage."

"Do you have children?" Ginny wondered how she could ever handle babies with a broken leg. Joy almost looked too young to be a mother, but Ginny was acutely aware that the older she got, the younger everyone else appeared to her.

Ginny knew instantly she'd said the wrong thing when a paroxysm of grief distorted Joy's face. "I lost my baby in the accident. I was six months pregnant."

Ginny could have bitten her tongue. "I'm terribly sorry. Me and my big mouth."

Joy wiped her eyes with the edge of her sheet. "People are always going to talk about babies. I'll just have to get used to it."

Ginny nodded at Joy giving her a sympathetic smile. She

vowed to herself that she would carefully avoid the subject of children as long as they shared a room. She had had great difficulty in conceiving Donald and was unable to become pregnant again after that. A lifelong battle with endometriosis led eventually to a hysterectomy soon after Donald's birth. She'd always thought of herself as an earth mother type, and long before she met Leland, she'd decided to have at least four or five children. When she finally understood that she would never have a houseful of babies, it caused her to reevaluate her view of herself. She knew it wasn't currently popular to think of women as "baby machines," but in her large family, childbirth was still considered the pinnacle of creativity. She could never accept herself as a completely successful woman after her operation. But now she realized her experience was nowhere near as tragic as Joy's. She'd never lost a child, thank God, and she had a wonderful son.

Leland arrived, followed almost immediately by Dr. Whittaker. It was the first they learned the full extent of the damage to her knee. She landed on it in such a way as to shatter the head of both tibia and fibula, the bones in the lower leg. The doctor was going to have to piece them together like a jigsaw puzzle, using metal plates and screws as well as a piece of hip bone as a graft. He warned them it would be a long healing process.

"How long will she be in the hospital?" Leland asked him.

"Probably no more than a week. But she's in for a long recovery at home and will have to come back for daily therapy once it's healed sufficiently."

Dr. Whittaker, dark and square-jawed, seemed sympathetic, if not emotionally involved in her problem. His manner was pleasant but brisk, and he tapped his pen against the clipboard holding her medical records with poorly concealed impatience to be off to see his next patient.

"Well, I sure have messed up your retirement, haven't I?" Ginny said after the doctor left. "Some fun it will be taking care of me."

"Don't you worry about anything. We're damned lucky I'm going to be free to do it. And that we have good hospitalization."

"Amen to that."

Leland left to run some errands before the luncheon and Ginny called her sister Melba.

"Oh, honey," Melba wailed. "Leland called me last night about you. I couldn't believe it!"

"Could I get you to call everyone and tell them the party's off?"

"I think I've talked to everybody already. Haven't your ears been buzzing? The whole family's so upset. And don't you worry about the party. You just concentrate on getting better."

"You're a dear. Tell everybody I'm doing okay. But the doctor says I'll have to have a lot of therapy. Honestly, Melba, I feel like an idiot."

"Don't say that, Ginny. It could happen to anyone. You be good now and do as the doctor says."

Melba was the oldest of her sisters and more like a mother to her. She fussed and clucked over all her seven siblings as if she were solely responsible for them. She had lost her husband Mack to cancer two years earlier and had more time now than ever to be the mother hen.

Next, Ginny called Leland's office and spoke to Dottie Hyland, the receptionist. Dottie agreed to spread the word about the party being cancelled. "It's such a shame you'll miss the luncheon today."

"Yes," said Ginny crossing her fingers, "Leland's been looking forward to it so much. I'm really disappointed." She hated telling white lies, even when it was dictated by good manners.

Myrna Caulfield said she would be happy to call the neighbors, although she was certain they all realized the party was off. "Let us know what we can do to help."

Everyone wanted to help. Why couldn't someone wave a magic wand and have all this disappear? Her mind kept thinking what if? What if? Why couldn't she go back and start yesterday all over again?

Leland came back late in the afternoon and ordered an extra tray for dinner so they could eat together.

Joy was awake—she'd been asleep when Leland was there earlier—so Ginny introduced them.

Leland nodded hello. "Peas in a pod," he grinned, waving at their respective legs in traction.

"It feels more like a chain gang the way we're trussed up here," Joy retorted. "Nice to meet you."

"Glad to know Ginny has a congenial roommate. Helps pass the time."

"Well, how does it feel to be retired?" Ginny asked him.

"I can't believe I'm free," he exulted. "After all these years, not to have to go in Monday morning and face the hassle."

"But now you have to put up with me. How was the luncheon? Did you survive the accolades?"

Leland stood up, straightened his shoulders, and put his fist on his chest in the manner of a great orator. "This man," he intoned in a deep voice, "single handedly held the company together in times of strife. Without his brilliant expertise, we would not even exist today. In spite of the fact that we sabotaged every good idea he had for new products, he endured and put up with our petty squabbles and office backstabbing. He will be enshrined in the Dunedin Industrial Rubber Products Hall of Fame along with all the others who tried like hell to bring this company into the twenty-first century only to find we much prefer to keep the status quo as it has been for the past fifty years. Three cheers for Leland McAllister."

Ginny was pursing her lips, trying her damnedest not to laugh because she knew it would hurt. She was so relieved that Leland could joke about office politics now.

"By the way," she said, "I've a confession to make. I'd planned a surprise party for you tomorrow."

"Susan told me when I called. I suppose it's on account of me you fell. Otherwise you wouldn't have been on that ladder."

"Sure I would have. You know I can't stand dirty windows."

FIVE

Ginny couldn't have had a better roommate than Joy who was unfailingly cheerful and considerate. Once in a while when Ginny was reading or watching television and happened to glance her way, she'd notice Joy brushing away a tear. It was obvious she was thinking about the baby she lost because Joy would stroke her now flattened stomach as if unconsciously searching for some movement, some sign of life. But she never mentioned the baby again, and although there was no doubt she was grieving deeply for her lost child, she seemed determined not to discuss it.

Ginny wondered if it was wise to keep it all inside that way, but felt it was not up to her to initiate a conversation about the grief she was handling. She was such a sweet, dear girl, and Ginny couldn't help but admire her fortitude in the face of such tragedy. If Ginny could have had a daughter, Joy fit Ginny's ideal as closely as any young woman she'd ever met, and she was surprised to find she actually felt envious of Joy's mother. She hoped they might continue their friendship after they both were healed.

But then she had second thoughts. She wondered why a young woman would be interested in someone her age until she remembered Maggie Murcheson who had lived three houses down the street from them. Maggie was nearly thirty years older than Ginny, but they had a close and enduring friendship that lasted until Maggie's death last year. Maggie had been a combination friend/substitute mother/confidante, and Ginny remembered that Joy's mother lived in Oregon. Maybe she needed a substitute mother, too.

While they were eating their breakfast Saturday morning, a bearded, dark haired young man came into the room and walked over to Joy's bed. This must be Dave, Ginny thought, although Joy had said he wouldn't be back for another week.

"Is this your husband?" Ginny asked.

"Oh, no," Joy answered, "he's a friend, Tony Howard. This is Mrs. McAllister, Tony." Her eyes seemed wary, reticent.

"Do you mind if I pull the curtain so we can talk?" Tony began to pull the curtain between the beds before Ginny could answer.

"Sorry I can't leave the room," Ginny smiled self consciously and gestured at her leg. "I'll watch some TV." She turned on the wall set feeling embarrassed and uncomfortable. She tried to set the volume so that it would give them privacy but not keep them from hearing each other. She flicked through the channels but it was mostly cartoons. Finally she found CNN. But in spite of the TV noise and the fact that Joy and Tony were speaking in low voices, Ginny could not help but overhear fragments of conversation.

"Does Dave know?" Tony whispered hoarsely.

"Of course not."

"He still thinks the kid was his?"

"Yes, Tony."

"But you were thinking about leaving him."

"Not any more."

The Headline News was showing a clip of the police quelling rioters with nightsticks somewhere in the Far East. Ginny felt as though she, too, had been struck down. She closed her eyes and gripped the covers till her fingers began to ache.

Nothing more was said, at least that she could hear, and in a couple of minutes, Tony left without a word to either of them. As he passed by Ginny's bed on the way out of the room, he looked so sad Ginny didn't know whether to dislike him or pity him.

The curtain remained drawn, beyond the reach of either woman. Ginny was glad because she couldn't face Joy right then. She would have to pretend that she didn't hear the conversation, but she'd always been notoriously poor at trying to appear inscrutable.

Dr. Whitaker saved her unintentionally from any possible conversation with Joy, choosing that moment to come in and tell her that her surgery was scheduled for Monday morning. She could probably go home within three to four days if everything went well.

"And then what?"

"It's hard to say. Don't expect any miracles. It's going to be a long, tough fight, and your progress will be mainly up to you."

"Will I ever walk normally again?"

"You'll have to go through lots of therapy, but the eventual outcome should be pretty good if you work hard at it."

She loved the way he evaded answering her directly. Doctors. They were so scared of malpractice suits, you couldn't pin them down on anything.

She was dozing after lunch when someone touched her arm. She opened her eyes to see Susan bent over her, her dark eyes quizzical, her bright red lips pursed in concern.

"Ginny, are you okay?"

"Susan, what are you doing here?"

Susan stepped back and pulled Donald, who was standing behind her, to the bedside. "Well, we'd planned to come to the party, so I'd cleared our calendar of everything. As long as we were free anyway, we thought we might as well come down to see you." Was she simply insensitive or were her remarks carefully calculated? Ginny could never tell.

"Hi, Mom. How's the leg? Dad says you messed it up pretty good."

"Don't you think I have an exquisite sense of timing though? Just in time to celebrate your dad's retirement."

"You always did have a sense of the dramatic." Donald smiled as though he'd just made a witty remark. She thought he must be taking lessons from his wife.

"Maybe you'll relax a little about the housework now," Susan smiled sweetly.

She should know about that, thought Ginny, who cringed at the "relaxed" state of her daughter-in-law's housekeeping. She wondered how Donald could tolerate living in such clutter.

"Where's your father?"

"Parking the car. He'll be right up. We thought we'd take him to an early birthday lunch before we had to get back, so we can only spend a few minutes with you. Anyway, we don't want to tire you," Donald said.

"That's a lovely idea." Why couldn't they have thought of having lunch with her in the room? Leland knew they could order extra meals. Not only was the party cancelled, she was being excluded from any kind of celebration. How was it children could be so totally unaware?

When Leland appeared a few minutes later, she repeated what the doctor had said, and everyone agreed that they would be glad when the operation was over and she could begin to mend. They talked about Susan's law practice—she had a major role in some big takeover—and Donald's work which involved the construction of shopping centers. Leland again imitated some of the speech makers at his retirement luncheon and had them all laughing to Ginny's regret.

They weren't there more than thirty minutes before Susan stated that they simply must get to the restaurant if they were to get back to Cleveland on time. She was expecting an important phone call in the early evening, so they could not dawdle any longer.

A nursing assistant brought Ginny's lunch, a sorry-looking pork chop and cooked greens which looked like limp seaweed and tasted like it, too. The dessert was rice pudding which reminded her of her mother's rice pudding; was everything conspiring to see just how full of self pity it was possible to make her?

The assistant pulled back the curtain that had screened Joy's bed when she delivered her tray. Joy was looking forlornly at the ceiling, her eyes red from crying.

Ginny felt she had to say something now. It was too awkward to remain silent.

"I'd give anything for a Whopper and French fries right now. I know hospital food is supposed to be bad, but this is ridiculous."

Joy gave her a wan smile. "I don't feel like eating anyway, so it doesn't matter what they're serving."

"Hey, you need to keep up your strength. From what I hear, we're going to wish we were Olympic athletes by the time we get to therapy. They say it's rough."

"I guess so." She said it so listlessly that Ginny was alarmed.

She picked at her lunch, eating whatever didn't make her gag, trying to think of what more she could say to Joy. Joy remained silent and continued to stare at the ceiling.

Finally she felt she had to break the impasse. "I guess this has been a bad day for both of us. We're bound to have our ups and downs though. Maybe tomorrow it will look brighter." Only platitudes seemed to come out of her mouth. Why couldn't she ever think of something brilliant and astute to say?

"I wish my mom was here."

"I'm so sorry she can't be. But I'm probably around the same age as your mother. Maybe I could help some." She was simply amazed at herself since she normally went to great lengths to avoid any appearance of prying. But Joy was different. Joy was crying out for help.

She appeared to be considering Ginny's offer. She chewed on her lip and rolled and unrolled the hem of the sheet as if the rote movements could help her decide. After a few minutes, she reached for the bed controls and raised the head of her bed till she could look at Ginny more directly.

"I don't know if you heard my conversation with Tony this morning."

Ginny started to insist she had not but decided Joy would be more likely to be honest with her if she admitted that she had.

"I tried not to, but in such close quarters it was impossible not to hear."

Joy began to cry again, using her napkin to wipe her eyes. "I've done a terrible thing. Tony and I had gone together in high school, though after I met Dave I had eyes only for him. But Tony never gave up. He always kind of hung around the edges of my life, even after I married Dave, hoping I'd come back to him someday. One time Dave and I had a terrible fight just before he left town on business. I made the mistake of calling Tony up to cry on his shoulder. He was more than willing to comfort me, and I was so distraught I just lost my head.

"I found I was pregnant right after that, and there was no doubt in my mind that the baby was Tony's. I was even thinking about leaving Dave to live with Tony. Dave wanted us to wait till we had more money to have a family. He wasn't too pleased that I was pregnant. But Tony was crazy about the idea of the baby. Probably because he thought he'd get me back that way."

Ginny listened without comment. She never could get used

to the way young people viewed relationships today. It was kind of like musical chairs, with the sanctity of marriage vows holding little meaning.

"It was the accident that made me realize how much I love Dave," Joy continued. "In that instant when I saw that car come toward me and I thought I was going to die, I knew it was Dave that I wanted to be with. Now what am I going to do? Should I tell Dave the truth about the baby?"

Oh my, thought Ginny, what has she gotten herself into? What have *I* got myself into? There wasn't going to be an easy answer to this problem. Who was she to give advice on a situation as complicated as this? Her own courtship and marriage had been as uneventful as any could be. She'd met Leland her junior year in college, dated him the next two years, and married him the day after graduation, pretty much the accepted scenario for women at that time. She'd been a virgin on her wedding night which was not all that remarkable then. And they'd remained faithful all these years, their few crises centering around money problems and Donald's teenage rebelliousness.

She really wanted to help her, in spite of Joy's transgressions. There, but for a twist of fate, could be a daughter of my own, she thought. But how do you give advice if you've never experienced anything like it?

"Were you ever torn between whether or not you should tell Leland something? Something that might even cause him to leave you?" Joy asked.

Of course she'd never been in that position. But instead of answering Joy's question, she countered with a question of her own.

"Does Dave know about Tony?" It seemed to Ginny that Joy's course of action depended on the answer.

"No, he doesn't. He's away so much it was easy to see Tony without Dave knowing."

"Then why tell him the baby wasn't his? I don't think it's necessary for him to know that now. Maybe if it had lived," she saw Joy wince painfully, "it would have been different. Circumstances might have forced you to reveal it. But since you've decided that you really want Dave and will stay with him, why say anything?"

"Do you really think that's what I should do?" Joy wasn't persuaded yet.

Realizing that Joy desperately needed reassurance, Ginny made an instant decision to tell a white lie. The only way to convince her, she was sure of it, was to make up a fictional story to illustrate her point.

"When I was first married," she said, "I learned from a friend that my husband was having an affair with a woman in his office. I never let on that I knew. I learned later that the affair was over in a short time, but I was always sorry that I found out about it. I would much rather have remained ignorant, because try as I would, I could never get it entirely out of my mind.

"Why put that burden on Dave? The only thing you'll do is make him help you carry your guilt around."

"So what you're saying is that part of my punishment will be always knowing that I have this secret I can't share with him."

"That's the negative way of putting it. I'd say it's more like caring enough about him that you don't want to hurt him. And learning to be strong enough to handle your own problems."

Joy ran her fingers nervously through her frizzy hair as she struggled with the idea. She wiped her eyes again and stared down at her flattened stomach.

Ginny wanted to take her in her arms and comfort her, she looked so vulnerable and sad. Young people seemed to get themselves into such incredible messes these days. And it occurred to her that maybe her generation had failed them somehow.

"I guess what you're saying makes sense," Joy said at last. "If you say you'd rather not have known, then Dave would probably feel the same way. I don't think Tony would tell anyone, so I should just get on with my life."

"I don't think you'll regret it, Joy."

Joy managed a small smile at last. "I hated to unload on you like that, but I was desperate to talk to someone. My mom couldn't have helped me more."

"That's the nicest thing you could have told me." Ginny couldn't believe how much the compliment lifted her from her own depression.

Six

Leland returned by two, saying that Donald and Susan had headed back to Cleveland.

"Where did you go for lunch? What did you have?"

"We went to Burgundy Hill. Sure, it was nice, but it wasn't the same without you."

I'll bet, thought Ginny. They no doubt had prime rib while I had those disgusting chopped greens.

"Hey, little lady, what do you think you're doing falling off some damn ladder?" The voice overwhelmed the room as did the presence of Wally Washburn, Ginny's brother.

"Wally, for heaven's sake," Ginny said, "where did you come from?" Wally and his wife Constance lived in Mansfield about seventy miles north of Columbus.

Wally waddled up beside the bed, his three hundred pounds of flesh still bobbing from the effort of walking down the long hospital corridor. Constance trailed behind, as always, peeking over his shoulder at Ginny.

"Well, shoot, Ginny, we were coming anyway for the party." He acted as if he suddenly noticed Leland was there. "Oh, congrats, Leland, on getting yourself out of that place. Ginny here sure added some excitement to the occasion, didn't she?"

"Shut up, Wally. Don't give me a hard time," Ginny laughed. "I remember how you ruined Mom and Dad's vacation when you broke your arm playing ball."

Constance, quiet till now, said in her soft little voice, "And don't forget, Wally, how you got appendicitis the night Beth was in the school play so neither of us got to see her."

The bantering continued after Ginny introduced her brother and his wife to Joy. Then Melba came, her widowed sister, so that the small room radiated body heat even though the air conditioning was on.

The room reverberated with the chatter and laughter of the garrulous Washburns. Ginny was soon exhausted and wished they would all leave.

She kept signaling Leland with her eyes. It took him a while to catch on, but at last he said, "Why don't we all go over to the house for a while. I think Ginny could stand a nap."

Blessed peace. The silence was tangible after they all left, wrapping her in blissful tranquility and she was soon asleep.

Ginny felt better Sunday morning after a fairly good night's rest. It was Leland's birthday, and she wanted to be in reasonably good shape for him. She'd bought him a new gardening cart which was hidden behind the vast old furnace in the basement. There was no way now to wrap up the box or get a card. She'd just have to tell him where it was.

He'd told her he'd go to church, and then come visit. He looked especially handsome when he arrived in his best summer weight gray suit. Leland never cared much about clothes. He dressed neatly but without much style for work, and when gardening or doing other chores, he looked like a street person in his ragged outfits he insisted served their purpose perfectly. He refused to get rid of clothes that were worn or out of style; he simply downgraded their functions to more casual occasions. Therefore he usually went shopping or spent weekends in ludicrously out-of-date outfits. But when he did on occasion dress up for church or a night out, Ginny would be caught by surprise every time by his attractiveness. It was as if she would forget how nice he could look.

"Hi, Ginny, hi, Joy." His eyes as cheery as his sky blue tie.

"Happy birthday, darling. You look terrific. Did I ever tell you how handsome you are?" She made a point to say so whenever he looked especially nice hoping he'd take the hint.

"You look pretty spiffy yourself."

"That's just lipstick. It's the first time in three days I've felt like bothering. And that's about all I can do to help you celebrate."

"Not to worry. I have a surprise." He retreated to the hall and came back pushing a hospital cart. "I thought the occasion deserved a little something special so I got permission to bring in a birthday meal.

"Voila!" He pulled off a large towel covering the cart to reveal three filled plates, three goblets, and a small crystal vase with a single rose. He put a plate and goblet on Joy's bedside tray and wheeled it across her bed, then Ginny's, then pulled out a bottle of white sparkling grape juice from a lower shelf, opened it, and poured some into the goblets. He pulled the cart containing his serving up to the chair beside Ginny's bed.

There was rare roast beef, scalloped potatoes, peas and mushrooms, croissants and butter.

"This is wonderful. Where on earth did it come from?"

"I guess I'll have to confess that Melba did this for me. The hospital staff was nice enough to warm it in the microwave when I got here. I kind of think they were a little miffed though."

"Let them be miffed. Their food is disgusting. Maybe they'll get the hint."

"Ha," said Joy. "You've got to be kidding. Anyway, it was sweet of you to include me."

"Oh, wait, I forgot." Leland reached under the cart and pulled out three bowls of salad and a bottle of salad dressing. "This isn't too elegant a way to serve the dressing I'm afraid."

"Honey, it's wonderful. Let's eat."

The meal was delectable, but then Melba, like all Washburns, was a splendid cook.

"Now for the finale," Leland said when they were finished. He went back out into the hall, and when he returned this time, he was carrying a cake covered with burning candles. "Happy birthday to me, happy birthday to me . . . ," he sang, and they ate large helpings of the chocolate cake, even Leland who usually disdained sweets. Ginny's spirits were so much better than they'd been since the accident. She saw herself as a true child of Cancer, vulnerable to wide mood swings which were usually difficult to conceal. Little things could stir her emotions, like this meal which made her almost euphoric. This little surprise party probably meant far more to her than the large one she'd planned could ever have meant to Leland.

As Leland was clearing the trays and putting the soiled dishes in a shopping bag he'd brought, a nurse and two orderlies came into the room.

"We're taking you down for some X-rays," the nurse told Joy.

"How can they do X-rays with my leg hung up like this?"

"Simple enough. We're just going to take you bed and all. You don't have to move a muscle."

"Thank God."

The room was small and it took some maneuvering for them to jockey Joy's bed around since it was in the far corner. But they finally managed to get it out, only bumping Ginny's bed twice. She wanted to tell the orderlies how clumsy they were, but there was no sense in spoiling the holiday mood of the party.

"That was a lovely surprise," she said when they were gone.

Leland put on a mock stern look. "You really should have gotten out of bed and fixed it yourself. Too much lollygagging here."

41

"Don't I wish. What you don't know is that I have enough food in the freezer for ten birthday parties. I'd been making things for your surprise party for weeks. Of course it's mostly sweets. We'd blow up like balloons if we ate it all." She took his hand and squeezed it, regretting that he'd had to arrange for his own birthday party.

"Well, you may want it when you get home. You're going to get damned tired of grilled cheese sandwiches," Leland grinned playfully.

"After all these years of marriage it's a sorry state of affairs that you still can't cook, Leland. Now that you're retired, we'll have to change some things." She said it tongue-in-cheek because it was her fault she never let him near the kitchen. She'd always thought of it as her domain. And she knew she'd be anxious to get back to preparing meals because it gave her so much pleasure.

"Hey, forget that. I'll pitch in now, but don't expect to see me in the kitchen again when you're up and about. That's still your realm."

What could she say? She couldn't argue the point. She did love to cook and really didn't want to give it up. It was going to be interesting to see how well Leland managed these next few weeks.

"Oh, Leland, I've got to tell you something now that Joy is out of the room." She loved sharing gossip with him. He enjoyed hearing about the liaisons and transgressions in the neighborhood as much as any woman she'd ever known.

She told him about Tony coming in and how upset Joy had been when he left.

"She finally, reluctantly, confided in me. It seems the baby was Tony's, not her husband's."

"And where, for God's sake, was her husband during all this?" Leland seemed genuinely concerned. He was becoming fond of Joy, too.

"Traveling for his job. They'd had a big fight. She used to go with Tony, who'd never lost interest in her. I guess he kind of made himself available, and when she confided in him about the blowup, things got out of hand."

"I'll say they did."

"She even thought of leaving her husband for him. But after the accident, she realized that she really loved Dave and wanted to stay with him."

Leland just shook his head. Ginny knew he was as shocked as she had been.

"I was really flattered when she asked me for advice. I was afraid she thought of me as somewhat archaic."

"Which you are." He said this with a deadpan expression.

"I think I was rather creative, to be honest." She knew Leland would get a kick out of the story she concocted for Joy.

"How's that?"

"I knew she wouldn't be impressed with anything I had to say unless I let on that I'd been through the same kind of thing. She wanted to know if she should tell her husband the truth about the baby. I said that she shouldn't. And then to back up my statement I told her that I learned long ago that you were having an affair . . ."

Ginny stopped mid-sentence when she saw the look of disbelief and horror on Leland's face.

"I . . . I made up this story . . ." she tried to explain, but Leland's expression left no doubt.

In her desire to entertain him, she'd stumbled onto a secret so unbelievable that she could scarcely accept it. For all their years of marriage, the idea of Leland being unfaithful had never occurred to her. She never had the slightest temptation to have an affair, and she had no suspicions whatever about him. Had she always been too trusting?

Leland seemed stunned. He took her hand in both of his, and with eyes that pleaded for understanding said, "That was years ago and didn't last any time at all. It was a girl in the office who came on to me when I was the most vulnerable. It happened when Donald was in trouble, and I was really at my lowest point. I just couldn't deal with things. I wasn't myself then, Ginny. It didn't mean anything."

"And I thought you were always faithful. I can't believe this." Although every inch of her body felt unresponsive and numb, tears began to wet her cheeks as if the deadness inside her was overflowing.

"Oh, Ginny, please, honey. I've never loved anyone but you. Put it out of your mind, it was nothing. We have so much to look forward to. Think about our wonderful future together now that I'm retired."

But the shock of this revelation on top of the pain and frustration over her broken knee made it too much to bear at this moment. It seemed as though her world had made such an abrupt turn in the past couple of days that it had left her ability to adjust to it all behind. Even though she knew her behavior was irrational, she couldn't help herself.

"Go home, Leland," she said. "I don't want to talk about it anymore."

"But we need to discuss it," he pleaded.

She shook her head and turned away from him to stare out the window. After a while he quietly gathered up the remains of the birthday lunch and left.

When he was gone, she realized how unreasonable she had been and wept anew. But her emotions seemed totally out of her control any more.

SEVEN

The surgery lasted four hours on Monday and was successful, and a week later Ginny returned home in an ambulance. Leland had brought one of the twin beds downstairs from the guestroom and set it up beside the dining room window that looked out over the backyard. On the drop leaf table next to the bed was a large bouquet of roses that he had gathered from his garden. He was trying so hard.

Although she'd tried to prepare herself mentally for the recovery period, it was worse than she'd imagined. She was glad Leland was home; she would have gone crazy if she'd been alone all day. They never mentioned his affair again, and the pain of learning about it was subsiding. But she knew it would always be there subtly between them like the film on a dirty window that reduces the normal brilliance of the colors on the other side.

Ginny felt herself sinking into a moroseness from the inactivity. Leland tried to keep up a cheerful banter, but soon she felt it was too much effort to match.

One morning, after she'd given herself a sponge bath and was using a mirror to comb her hair, she was shocked to realize she hardly recognized the face reflected there. Her hair, which she'd always kept tinted a soft chestnut brown, had grown out exposing an inch of gray at the roots. She'd lost weight, too, since her appetite was anything but aroused by Leland's attempts at cooking. Mostly he bought frozen dinners till she thought she'd choke if she had to eat another rubbery cubed steak. The only respite was when Melba brought in a meal. On one of her visits, Melba told her that Leland was very concerned about her. "He doesn't like the way you're losing weight, and he says you're barely talking to him any more."

"Well, he brought it on himself, you know." Ginny hadn't meant to talk about it; it had simply slipped out. But now that she'd opened the door, maybe it would help to discuss it with Melba. Her sister was a very nurturing kind of person, had been so ever since they were young. And the irony was that she'd been unable to have any children. Maybe that was why even now, Melba's attitude toward Ginny still had the faint overtones of a mother-daughter relationship.

"Why do you say that?" Melba asked. "He seems so attentive, and he worries himself sick about you."

"I found out that Leland had an affair."

"Recently?"

"No, back when Donald was still at home and in so much trouble."

"Has he seen her since?"

"He says not."

"That was sixteen years ago. My God, Ginny, that's ancient history. Why on earth are you so upset about it now?" Melba was frowning now.

She couldn't believe Melba was saying this.

"Because I just found out about it," Ginny said, "and I'd gone all those years thinking he was faithful to me when he wasn't. That's hard to accept."

"Oh, for heaven's sake, Ginny, snap out of it. You should be damn thankful you have a husband. If I had Mack back, he could have an affair if he wanted so long as he came back to me every night. All I've got to say to you is if you still have him, do everything in your power to keep him. Don't drive him off.

Cherish him.”

Ginny said nothing. She couldn't seem to throw off the sense of betrayal she felt even though she knew she was overreacting. Perhaps if she had learned about it at a different time when the rest of her life was on an even keel she could have handled it better.

That evening she and Leland watched an R-rated movie he'd rented. As she watched the love scenes, she realized that part of her discontentment came from not being able to make love for the past month. Leland was surely frustrated too, although he never mentioned it. But the way she'd been acting, how would he dare?

When the movie was over, Ginny put her arm around his neck when he kissed her good night.

“Why don't you come to bed with me for a while,” she pecked at his nose. “It's been a long time.”

“You're right. It has. But I don't see how we can do it without hurting you.”

“Very, very carefully.” She gave him her wickedest smile.

He pulled on his earlobe for a minute, seeming to be torn between desire and caution. At last he undressed and slipped in beside her.

He was very gentle as he stroked her body, and she realized how much she'd missed his touch. Since they had been unable to make love for so long, their kisses and caresses quickly aroused them both. Ginny couldn't do much but lie on her back like a beached whale with the full cast on her leg. Leland, so afraid of hurting her, and forced into such an awkward position to avoid putting pressure on her broken knee, nearly fell off the bed as he attempted to consummate the act. He was only partially successful, but they ended up doubled over in a paroxysm of laughter at the ludicrousness of their lovemaking in spite of the less than satisfactory result. Maybe it had not entirely satisfied their sexual longings, but it did much to relieve the tension between them.

Her mood improved after that, but her spirits were still low. The tediousness of the days overwhelmed her, wearing away her energy and good humor. She was scheduled to start her daily trips to the hospital for therapy soon, and she'd heard stories about how difficult it could be.

One evening during dinner, he told her he had a surprise for her.

"Remember how we talked about the possibility of moving to Florida?" he asked. "I got to thinking that what we need is a complete change of scenery, a whole new start."

"Are you talking about next year?"

"No, I'm talking about right now, as soon as the doctor will let you travel."

"Be realistic, Leland. I'm not going to feel like running around looking at houses for a long time."

"I know that. That's why I've asked Susan to go down with me this weekend and look at property. If I can find a suitable place and have it all fixed up and ready for you, wouldn't you consider it?"

"Oh Lord, Leland, I don't know. Don't you think we should wait?"

"No, I don't. I know how depressed you've been. And if you have to spend the winter cooped up here, you'll really hit bottom. Just think how great it would be to have a place overlooking the water with lots of sunshine all year round. You could sit out on the beach, and I know we'd both be a lot happier." He stared into space as if envisioning waves lapping on the shore. A smile spread across his face as he leaned back and clasped his hands together across his chest in a gesture of satisfaction.

His arguments were valid. She was dreading the winter

months already, with the treacherous ice and snow. She didn't want to be a prisoner in the house for weeks on end. But she had a lot of reservations about someone else picking out a house for her, *especially* Susan. Their tastes were not at all alike. And what was her motivation for doing it anyway? Surely altruism was not one of her attributes.

"I can't help but think Susan wants to get us far enough away so they won't have to feel guilty about not visiting us but once in a blue moon." As soon as she said it she knew it sounded spiteful. She could have bitten her tongue. Sometimes it felt as if her mouth was not attached to her brain. Did something shake loose when she fell off the ladder?

Leland sighed deeply and sat on the edge of her bed. "Look, I know this is a tedious business, and you must be at the end of your rope. That's why I'm anxious to give you a change of scenery. And, truthfully, Ginny, it's for both of us. This is getting me down as much as it is you."

What could she say after that. "When do you leave?"

"I'm driving up to Cleveland Friday afternoon where I'll pick her up after work. We leave on the 6:20 flight. We'll get back to Cleveland late Sunday so I'll spend the night with them and drive home Monday."

"You seem to have it all planned out, before discussing it with me. Looks like I'm being railroaded here." She tried to keep a light tone to show that she was kidding, even though she was not.

"I had to make sure I could work it all out before it made sense to discuss it. I know you won't regret it, Ginny."

"If you say so." She had an empty feeling in her stomach, as if what little control she had over her life had been finally and irrevocably taken from her. Not that she ever had any great input; Leland always made most of the major decisions which had been fine with her. But they used to discuss things in great detail, at least giving her some part in the decision-making process.

Melba stayed with her while Leland was gone, and Ginny was delighted not only to have her company, but for her delicious meals as well.

Sunday night Leland called from Cleveland. "We've been so rushed, I didn't have a minute to call you till now. I've got a wonderful surprise, Ginny. I'll tell you about it when I get home tomorrow."

"It looks like he's done it," she told Melba after she ended the phone call. "Apparently he's found a place to buy."

"What's it like? Is it on the water?" Melba sounded excited.

"He won't tell me a thing till he gets back." Ginny, though she tried, was unable to match her sister's enthusiasm.

"That's a man for you. Keep up the suspense, draw out the intrigue."

"Melba! You told me to cherish him, remember?" Ginny exclaimed laughing.

"Did I ever say men were perfect? You can love them even when you know all their faults. In fact I think it's easier to love somebody when you understand their quirks. Who wants somebody who hasn't got any? Boring, boring."

Leland was home before noon on Monday. Ginny couldn't remember when he'd looked so pleased with himself. He brought each of them a chambered nautilus with a little plastic display stand.

"It's beautiful," Ginny said, admiring the shell's graceful shape.

"Almost as beautiful as our new condominium," he said, pulling a brochure out of his suitcase. "Look, here are the room plans." The brochure was for Tranquility Gardens. "One of Siesta Key's most delightful condominium communities overlooking the Gulf of Mexico."

"I thought you were in Sarasota."

"It's an island right off Sarasota, across the inland waterway, and it has the most beautiful beach you've ever seen—pure white sand."

"Sounds expensive."

"Usually it is. But this builder was in financial difficulty—he had cash flow problems—and he was practically giving these places away. Comparatively speaking, of course. We've got one terrific bargain."

"But how can we do it when you haven't sold our house?"

"On a contingency basis. I don't have to close the deal till we've sold this place."

Ginny studied the floor plan and tried to come to grips with what was happening. It had seemed unreal before—kind of a distant dream—the way they used to speculate about the future when they were young. It was a game they played, a way to deal with the realities of everyday life and a lack of money, so there were never any genuine expectations. This was like one of those pie-in-the-sky flights of fancy, only it was *real* this time. And she wasn't ready for it.

"This looks great," said Melba looking at the plans, filling the void left by Ginny's silence.

Leland smiled with a satisfaction that Ginny hadn't seen since his last promotion, years ago. "I've saved the best for last."

"Well?" asked Ginny.

"The builder sold me the furnishings from the model dirt cheap. I swear I got them for practically nothing. Since only a couple of units were left, he didn't need the model any more."

"Furnishings? What are you talking about? What about all our things here?"

"Ginny, honey, most of it's worn out, and it would cost too much to move anyway. Besides, we want nice looking stuff that's appropriate for Florida."

"Oh, Leland, what about the family things?" She knew they didn't mean much to him. A table was a table as far as he was concerned. That it once belonged to her grandmother made little difference.

He scowled, picked at a fingernail, and finally said, "Well, if you want to keep a few special pieces, I guess we could do that."

"What about the piano?"

"It's out of the question. It would cost a mint to move and there isn't room for it anyway. You hardly ever play it."

"But it was my grandfather's."

"Come on, Ginny, be reasonable. You know it's in bad shape. If you played a lot it would be different. Take some of your favorite knickknacks, tables, or dressers, and let's get rid of the rest."

It was settled then. Leland had already made up his mind. She didn't even ask what the new furniture looked like. She'd find out soon enough.

Leland was oblivious to her misgivings. "It looks like we're on our way," he said cheerily. "This will be great for you, Ginny. Swimming in the Gulf will help heal your leg. You won't have to worry about slipping on ice. It'll keep both of us young. Once you get used to the idea of a new start, you'll love it."

EIGHT

The next few weeks were a blur of trips to physical therapy sessions. It was so painful she wanted to tell them to forget it, to leave her alone. She'd learn to hobble around for the rest of her life. But common sense and Leland prevailed.

Meanwhile, Leland talked with realtors who poked into every corner of the house to determine its market value. Ginny hated the way they would point out its drawbacks instead of its charms; in fact, she was incensed at some who seemed to delight in finding fault.

After a week of that, Leland told her he'd decided to sell it himself, and she was relieved not to have to listen to any more negative comments. It did mean, however, that they had to be available at any time to show it, and she couldn't wear her housecoat most of the morning as she had been doing.

Once their sign was up, they had a fairly steady stream of lookers, but no serious offers were made. Even though Ginny felt relief that the sale of the house wasn't imminent, she couldn't understand why others didn't find it as appealing as she always had.

Possible buyers seemed to nitpick. Instead of acknowledging the pleasant coziness of the breakfast nook, they'd complain that it was too small or that the kitchen wasn't "efficient." And everyone pointed out that one-and-a-half baths simply wasn't enough.

Three weeks after they began to show the house, the doorbell rang one morning while Leland was working in the backyard. His beautiful garden was one of their strongest selling points so he wanted to keep it in the best possible condition. Ginny was reading and put aside her book. She was pretty adept at the crutches now, at least on flat surfaces.

When she opened the door, she was astonished to see Joy Wentowski, her roommate from the hospital. Joy seemed equally surprised to see her.

"Mrs. McAllister! I had no idea you lived here." She looked healthy and happy and apparently her leg had healed with no complications.

"Well, for heaven's sake, come on in." Ginny made a little gesture with her crutch waving Joy into the house. "What are you doing here?"

"Dave and I want to buy a house, and we particularly love this older area. I was driving around the neighborhood when I saw the sign and decided to take a look. Are you buying something smaller or going to one floor?"

"No, dear. We're moving to Florida. Leland found a condominium in Sarasota right on the beach."

"How wonderful." Joy exclaimed. "How's your leg?"

"So-so. I don't think it will ever be perfectly normal, but I do hope I can scrap these crutches pretty soon. You look like you're doing great."

"I've healed well enough."

Ginny wondered if her spirit had healed, too.

"Say," Joy continued, "would this be a convenient time for me to look at the house? I can come back if it isn't."

"It's as good as any. Come on, and I'll give you the grand tour."

She took Joy through the rooms, pointing out the things she thought would appeal to her like the original oak woodwork and floors, and the ornamental mantelpiece.

"What a lovely piano," Joy exclaimed. "Aren't you the lucky one."

Ginny couldn't answer her at first; her throat tightened up every time she thought about it. It was symbolic of everything she was having to give up.

"I'm afraid we'll have to sell it," she said. "There won't be room for it in the new place."

When they got to the kitchen, Ginny began to apologize, but Joy cut her short. "I think it's charming. I get tired of these sleek modern ones that have no personality."

Ginny sent her upstairs to look around by herself, and she came back down extolling the "cozy" bedrooms and the "darling old-fashioned" bathroom. She was the first person to go through the house who didn't criticize something. Ginny hoped she wasn't just being polite.

Leland greeted Joy warmly when they went out to the garden.

"I can't wait to bring Dave over," she told him, "I know he's going to love it as much as I do."

The Wentowskis came back on Saturday morning after Dave returned from Michigan, and he was just as enthused as Joy. They made an offer right then so close to the asking price that Ginny and Leland accepted it immediately.

Joy grabbed Ginny and hugged her, almost knocking her off balance. "I'm so excited I can't stand it," she giggled.

It was a moment of two extremes for Ginny: one of great elation that her home would be in the loving hands of Joy and Dave. On the other hand, it was a moment of sad finality, too. Her beloved house no longer belonged to them, and it would take a while to come to terms with that. But she was careful only to reveal her happy side. She wouldn't spoil this moment for the Wentowskis for anything.

They told the young couple that they couldn't move until the doctor released Ginny from his care which would probably be late October. Joy said that would work out well. Their lease would be up October 31. The sale seemed preordained.

Ginny graduated to a cane in early September and began to decide what items she could take to Florida. It was one of the hardest things she ever had to do, going through closets and cupboards item by item, determining the future of each plate, vase or towel while Leland constantly reminded her that space was at a premium in the condo.

She found a spiral notebook full of poetry she'd written years ago when she was young on the back of a closet shelf. She'd tried to express her feelings in verse, but when she reread the poems now, they seemed strident. She debated for a day whether or not to keep the notebook, but finally threw it out.

She called Susan and asked her if she wanted to come down and see if there was anything she and Donald would like before they had a garage sale.

"Thanks anyway," Susan replied. "We have such different tastes in furnishings, I don't believe your pieces would go too well with our things."

She'd known better than to ask Susan, but she couldn't dispose of family items without at least making the gesture. She wondered if Susan would even mention it to Donald, and if he had any sentimental feelings about any of it. She was tempted to call him at his office and put the question directly to him. But she thought better of it.

She called Joy then, to ask if they wanted to buy any of the furniture.

"We don't need much," she answered, "and buying the house is going to take about everything we've got right now. But I've been thinking about that piano. I believe you said you weren't taking it with you?"

"Leland says there isn't room."

"I couldn't pay you outright for it, but could we buy it in

monthly installments?"

"Joy, if you want it, we can work out any kind of arrangement that would suit you. I'd be so happy to know it's still here." If she hadn't needed a cane, she would have danced around the room. It was such a relief to know that the piano as well as the house would be in their hands. It was going to make it much easier to give them both up.

Dr. Whittaker discharged her from his care on October 12. She was still using a cane, but he said she could do away with it whenever she felt secure enough, and to continue to do her exercises. "It will probably never be one hundred percent the way it was, but you've come a very long way, Ginny, and you'll probably gain even more motion over the next few months. Considering the damage that was done, the outcome could have been not nearly as good."

"Thank you. I feel blessed it wasn't any worse." She knew that she was lucky, that she could have been severely crippled, but that lame leg had altered forever her concept of herself; she felt as if she'd added a dozen years to her age the day she fell.

The following weekend they had an overwhelmingly successful yard sale. Ginny couldn't believe the way people fought over things she'd nearly thrown out. Leland was the canny one. He knew that anything would sell if shoppers believed it was a bargain. What few things remained, they gave to Goodwill.

The house wasn't the same with most of the furniture gone. Its defects were more obvious now that they were exposed. And it felt strange and unfamiliar to have all that empty space. Ginny was finally anxious to leave, not to get to Florida, but to escape from the vacuum created by the sale.

The movers came on the twenty-eighth and loaded up the few remaining tables and chests and Ginny's favorite chair.

She called Melba from the motel that night. "We'll be on our way bright and early. Lord, but I'm going to miss you, Melba. You've got to visit us often."

"You couldn't feel worse than I do. I'll figure out a way. But you know I have a problem with Mickey."

Mickey was a mongrel dog Melba adored and doted on as if he were a child. She refused to leave him at a kennel.

"Well, figure something out. Who's more important, Mickey or me?"

Melba laughed. "I knew you were going to ask me that some day. You'll have to figure it out for yourself, kiddo."

That night Ginny dreamed she was wandering around the upstairs of her old house and fell down the steps. As she lay helplessly at the bottom, calling out for help, her voice echoed in the empty rooms, and she realized there was no one to come to her rescue. She awoke in a panic, drenched with sweat, and hurriedly turned on the bedside light as she was momentarily disorganized and couldn't remember where she was.

"Ginny?" Leland awoke when the light came on. "What's wrong?"

"Just a bad dream, honey. Go back to sleep," she said, trying to keep her voice calm. But she wasn't able to sleep herself for the rest of the night.

NINE

Three days later they were in Sarasota. Leland drove over the bridge that linked the island of Siesta Key to the mainland and down Higel Avenue. The street was bordered by palms and Australian pines and other tropical foliage so thick that most of the homes were hidden from sight. They passed through Siesta Village, a small shopping area and, suddenly, around a bend in the road, they were greeted by a shimmering white beach bordering the Gulf. The water was a patchwork of electric blue and turquoise as the sandy bottom reflected back the sun's rays at varying depths. Ginny had to admit it was a spectacular sight.

Beyond the public beach, rows of high rise condominiums were lined up along Midnight Pass Road obscuring the view of the Gulf for all but the privileged few who could afford to live there. Ginny tried to imagine what the island must have been like before the developers came.

She'd seen the wildlife preserve on Sanibel Island and supposed it had been like that, overgrown and wild, teeming with shore birds, silent except for the raucous cry of gulls and the sound of the wind and the waves on the shore. Soon Leland pulled into a drive that led to an eight-story building. The sign on the rather elaborate entrance was in script: Tranquility Gardens. There were some gardens here and there to lend credence to the name; roses here, azaleas there. There were hibiscus bushes surrounding the lawn in rainbow colors and trees with deep magenta blooms that looked exactly like orchids.

They pulled into a space marked six-fourteen under one of the long rows of carports and got out of the car, stretching their aching muscles. "Let's go look at our place before we unload," Leland told her. He took her arm and steered her toward the building, its white stucco glistening in the sun. Long walkways ran from one end to the other across each floor giving access to the individual units. Two outdoor elevators rose in columns at either end, and they rode one up to the sixth floor.

When he unlocked the door of their condo and threw it open grandly, in a typically Leland-like gesture, her first impression was light. Almost overwhelming light.

This was so unlike their old house where the rooms were dimly lit by the few sun rays that managed to filter through the massive oaks that hovered over the Dutch colonial. Even on the brightest days it had been necessary to turn on a lamp to read. But there was something comforting, like an enveloping presence, about the semi-gloom of the seventy-five-year-old house.

Here the sunlight was unrelieved, intensified by the white shag carpeting and the daffodil yellow davenport and chair. The huge picture window that covered one entire wall of the living room seemed to gather in the brightness, pulling in the piercing reflections from the Gulf waters and the iridescent whiteness of the sand, magnifying them to almost unbearable brilliance.

"Well, what do you think?" Leland walked over to the window and stood with his back to the view, illuminated from behind so that his hair, now longer and grayer than six months ago, appeared as a glowing halo. His features appeared serene, his eyes calm. Only the fact that he pulled at his earlobe gave away the fact that he was not completely self-assured.

Ginny needed some time before she could answer truthfully. She was so taken by surprise by the contrast between this home and the one in Columbus she didn't know how to react. All she could do was blurt out, "You could go blind in here," and instantly regretted it. He was waiting to be told how wonderful it was, but she couldn't do it. At least not yet. So she said, "Leland, you're a wonder," which said everything and nothing.

"I knew you'd love it," he smiled, relieved. "When Susan and I saw this, we knew immediately it was the perfect place."

She limped over to the nearest chair which faced the whole panorama of beach and sea, and from their sixth-floor vantage point she watched the beach walkers as they strode purposefully in both directions near the edge of the water, bright little spots of color against the startlingly white sand. That looks like a pleasant enough pastime for a two-week vacation, she thought, but do I really want this for the rest of my life?

A sense of panic gripped her, and she felt she'd been cut loose from everything that connected her to her former world. Her family was twelve hundred miles away, the home she'd lived in and loved for so many years occupied by someone else. Her friends were all in Ohio. She felt adrift, directionless. She wanted to cry.

Instead she tried to smile, berating herself for being such a damn fool when Leland was so proud of what he had done.

"This is a lovely view." She couldn't deny that the sweep of beach and sand and sky was truly magnificent. If they'd been on vacation, she would have written her friends extolling the scenery; but this was permanent, and that was a whole different matter. View just wasn't enough for a lifetime.

"Come see the kitchen." Leland held out his hand to help her up. "You're really going to love it."

He led her toward the front of the condo where the kitchen looked out over the parking lot. It too sparkled, only slightly less than the living room since there was only one window in the breakfast area. The cupboards were European style, the doors and drawers in white without ornamentation. The countertop was also white marble, and each appliance was the latest and fanciest model, including the built-in microwave. Most women would kill for such a kitchen, she thought.

But Ginny was struck by the sterility of the room that looked more like a hospital laboratory to her. She thought of her kitchen in Columbus, somewhat dowdy and more than a little outdated, but warm and inviting with its ceiling-high cupboards, old porcelain sink and drain board, and the thirty-year-old stove. Perhaps it wasn't stylish, but it was the heart of the house, its most used room where they would linger in the breakfast alcove, watching the birds and squirrels vie for the seeds on the bird feeder that hung outside the window.

She could never feel that comfortable here. It seemed to her not quite natural to be living six stories off the ground.

She tried hard to appear enthused. "Just look at all these doodads on the refrigerator," she said, examining the ice cube and water dispenser on the door. "They didn't leave out a thing in here, did they? You get the feeling that meals could get fixed without the help of a human hand. Just push a few buttons and presto! there's your dinner."

"You're close," Leland laughed, obviously pleased. "Everything you need to make your life as easy as possible."

She felt a tinge of nausea at the idea of a totally effortless life. "It needs a little color in here," she changed the subject. "Maybe I could hang some bright paper to jazz it up a bit."

"Oh please, Ginny, stay off the ladders. One smashed-up knee is enough."

She could feel her face flush. "All right, Leland, calm down. I can hire it done." She was used to doing those kinds of things herself, although she hadn't thought about having to use a ladder. She never wanted to get near one again.

"Come on," said Leland, assuming the manner of a tour guide now that he apparently was reassured that Ginny approved of the condo. "Let me show you the rest of the place."

He led the way down the hall to the two bedrooms and bathrooms. The bedrooms, too, were filled with reflected light, intensified by the white carpet and white walls. There was a minimum of furniture, beds made of mattresses and springs on frames flanked by chrome and glass night stands. They were made up with yellow linens and spreads that matched the living room furniture.

Ginny had at least convinced Leland that they should not sell the few pieces of furniture that had been handed down from older generations of their families, so the cherry marble-topped dresser that had been her grandmother's, his grandfather's tall chest, and a few assorted tables and chairs were on the road somewhere between Ohio and Florida. Perhaps when those arrived, this place might remotely resemble a home. She prayed it would.

The master bath and hall bath, like the kitchen, though well appointed, had little charm. She hoped that brightly colored towels and pictures might give them some character.

"That's it. You've seen it all now. It's the nicest place on the beach in our price range." He looked at her questioningly, expecting confirmation.

She'd never lied to Leland. She couldn't lie to him now. So instead of saying what she knew he was waiting to hear, she said, "Let's christen it," putting her arms around him and holding him close. Her knee ached terribly, and she was tired, but she wanted to reassure him she was happy. This was the only way to do so without lying.

They pulled the miniblinds shut, Ginny experiencing a surge of relief as the sunlight was finally subdued, and made love in the king-sized bed. They both fell asleep immediately afterwards.

When Ginny awoke with a start an hour later, for a brief moment again she didn't remember where she was.

It was five days before the movers arrived with their household goods, and they had to eat all their meals out. She'd always thought eating out was a treat, but it became an onerous chore now. They soon found that most of the good restaurants had long waiting lines as early as 4:30 in the afternoon. And only the high priced places, which they couldn't afford, took reservations.

When the moving van arrived on Friday, Ginny was elated to see her few pieces of well-loved furniture and the boxes filled with the decorative items and dinnerware that she'd owned for years. These would go a long way into making this place her own. It was late in the day by the time everything was unloaded and brought up to their condo by elevator. Boxes and barrels cluttered the living room and kitchen, but Ginny's spirits were high.

"Let's leave everything as it is tonight and unpack in the morning," Leland suggested. "It's too late to start now."

"I've at least got to get some of the kitchen things out. I don't think I can stand another fast food breakfast. Why don't you go get some groceries for tomorrow."

She awoke early the next day, anxious to put the house in order. First she made an extravagant breakfast of juice, grapefruit, omelet, English muffins, bacon and coffee; their first meal there deserved a little celebration. When she began to set the table in the kitchen, the view of the parking lot struck her as less than appealing, so she carried it into the living room to be eaten on the drop leaf table in front of the picture window.

She woke Leland, who uncharacteristically was sleeping late these days, and they lingered over their meal, torn between wanting to get the house straightened up and dreading the job.

It took them most of the day to unpack all the boxes and barrels and put everything away. Ginny was sure that she'd sold or given away eighty percent of their belongings, but now it seemed they still had an inordinate amount of things to be stowed in closets and cupboards.

"We may have to have another sale," Leland said, as he tried to find space for some tablecloths in a linen closet that was already packed too tightly.

"Absolutely not. I'll find room in my dresser drawers or something, but I've already pared it down as far as I'll go. Maybe we'll have to rent storage space, but I'll be darned if I'll get rid of one more thing." She surprised herself at her determination.

In the kitchen, she had more space than ever before. She grudgingly admitted that a modern kitchen was efficient to work in even it if lacked character. But she missed their cozy breakfast nook and the bird feeder outside the window.

Leland had bought a couple of steaks the day before and they enjoyed a leisurely supper in the living room while they watched a dramatic sunset of brilliant colors.

"That is spectacular," Ginny said as the last tiny curve of the fluorescent orange ball that made up the sun disappeared into the calm sea, leaving behind clouds ablaze with reflected color.

"The tradition here is to rate the sunsets on a scale of one to ten. I'd say that rates at least a nine."

"If that's a nine, I can't imagine what a ten would be."

Leland reached across the table and put his hand over hers. "It's going to be wonderful. I know we're going to love it here."

Ginny smiled, saying nothing. She gazed about the room now that they'd finished unpacking. Her favorite vases, figurines and Majolica plates were displayed on the tables, and their familiar paintings were on the walls. The grandfather clock Leland had bought for their fifteenth wedding anniversary was in the small foyer, and the cherry drop leaf table that they were eating on had come on the moving van. A smaller antique table was between the model's davenport and chair, and she had cajoled

Leland into letting her put her chair in the living room, though on a trial basis. It was a wingback swivel rocker covered in a muted floral print. It didn't actually clash with the new furniture, but seemed anachronistic in these surroundings.

Yet Ginny felt it was the chair that gave the living room a touch of hominess. She was determined not to let Leland relegate it to the bedroom. Otherwise this room would never be hers. As it was, it would forever suffer from a split personality, a constant reminder of the sharp division of her life between "then" and "now."

TEN

Now that she was settled, Ginny wanted to get on with it and meet her neighbors and get involved in the community in some way. But the other condominiums on their floor seemed to be unoccupied.

"Where is everybody?" she asked Leland.

"They come down just for the winter. A few come before Christmas, but most after the first of the year."

"How am I supposed to meet people?"

"There are some other year-round residents—just not on our floor. I was told the women have a kaffee klatsch every Monday morning. Why don't you go?"

The following Monday Ginny went to the clubhouse at nine and found a half dozen women already there. By the time the meeting began there were fifteen. It seemed that their main goal, other than socializing, was to raise money for improvements around the condominium grounds. They were planning a bazaar for early December, and everyone was involved in making things to sell. Many of the ladies were knitting or crocheting something at the moment. Ginny was amazed at how they could work so rapidly, the crochet hook flashing in and out of the looped yarn, without seeming to pay the slightest attention to what they were doing. Others sat clicking their knitting needles as long scarves or afghans trailed from their laps. Ginny could do none of that.

Doris Leopold, who chaired the meeting, introduced Ginny

as the newest resident. The others nodded with indifference in her direction.

"Now what are we going to do with our proceeds this time?" Doris asked next.

"I think we ought to buy more statues," said one woman without even looking up from her crocheting.

Ginny couldn't believe she was serious. There were already far too many tacky statues about the grounds, from Grecian maidens carrying vessels on their shoulders to lions roaring silently to the sky. They were ludicrous and detracted from the otherwise innocuous high rise. Why weren't the flowers enough for them?

"No. We need to buy an organ for the clubhouse," another woman huffed. "We already have enough statuary." Right on! Ginny thought.

"But only a few people could play it," a woman in the back row argued. "Why buy something so expensive for so few?" She looked up from her knitting long enough to glare at the woman who suggested it.

"Because they could entertain at our parties," said the first woman sharply, as if any fool would have known that.

The discussion went on heatedly with several more suggestions. For every idea, someone had a negative comment. The arguments escalated and tempers rose, and if Ginny had been sitting in the last row and could have slipped out gracefully, she would have done so. But she was sitting right up front in the middle of the maelstrom. She wondered why Doris didn't bring the meeting to order, but she seemed content to let them fight it out. The meeting finally ended in a stalemate, and the decision was postponed till the next meeting. Ginny couldn't imagine how they would ever come to any kind of agreement.

When she finally was able to slip away, she hurried back home. Leland was out golfing with three other men from

Tranquility Gardens, so she busied herself washing already clean windows till he returned for lunch.

"How was your meeting?" he asked as they sat down to eat.

"I'm not going back."

"Why not? I thought you were anxious to meet people."

"I am. But all they did was fight over how to spend their bazaar money. It was ridiculous. Tranquility Gardens, my foot."

"What are you going to do then? Maybe you ought to take up golf."

"I don't think so. Not with my bad knee."

He shrugged and went on eating. She wasn't going to get much help from him.

Ginny began to walk the beach in the mornings, before it got too hot, looking for shells. She discovered Turtle Beach at the south end of the island where she could find the most, partly because fewer people went there and partly because the end of the beach next to Midnight Pass seemed to catch the majority of shells before waves could carry them further north.

It became a treasure hunt as she looked for the rarer shells there at the island's tip. There was a small park at the entrance to Turtle Beach that had picnic tables and play areas for children. Across the parking area, large dunes topped by sea oats screened the view of the Gulf until one climbed the few steps that led over the top and down the other side. From there the beach sloped gently down to the shore. It wasn't the pure white quartz sand that graced Crescent and Siesta beaches farther north on the island, but shells were far more plentiful. At the southernmost point of the key, storms pushed up mounds of sand and shells. She liked to sit on top of a pile and sort through the broken pieces to find the few still intact. She got books out of the library to identify them, and she began to be selective, looking especially for perfect whelks, cone shells, olives, and cat's eyes. It was therapeutic for her, easing her loneliness and her sense of dislocation. She gathered bags of shells without the slightest idea what she would do with them. But she couldn't give it up; they were like precious icons.

In searching for the perfect shell, it was as though she were sifting through the detritus of her life, discarding the broken pieces and imperfect shapes like her accident and Leland's affair in order to find the part worth preserving. She was still hurting physically and emotionally from these incidents, and she knew she had to "throw them away" or put them behind her, the way she did the shells she didn't want to keep.

Thanksgiving week came, and although Leland offered to take her to a restaurant, she insisted on cooking a turkey for the two of them. It was going to be a hard day to get through. Normally Susan and Donald came down from Cleveland, and most of her family gathered at their house for a huge meal to which everyone contributed. She couldn't bring herself to buy a turkey under fifteen pounds although she knew they would be eating leftovers forever. But she was sure that little birds just didn't taste as good.

She made all the trimmings from sweet potato casserole to both pumpkin and mincemeat pies, and they ate in front of the window in desultory silence. It was a rare rainy day, and somehow the gloom seemed more pronounced here than it did in Ohio in years past when it rained on Thanksgiving Day. They had eaten early and were watching football on TV when the phone rang. It was Carla Hoff, her former next-door neighbor.

"I have some bad news for you," she told Ginny.

"What?" Her stomach did a flip flop.

"It's your house. There was a fire." Carla said.

"Oh, my God. How bad?" Ginny couldn't believe it.

"It's pretty well destroyed."

"What about Joy and Dave?"

"They're okay. They got out. But the house won't be the same."

"What happened?" Ginny asked.

"Dave was redecorating the kitchen. He'd put paint remover on the cabinets, and when he plugged in the electric sander preparing to sand them down, it caused a spark, and the kitchen went up like a torch. He got out in time and was really lucky not to have been seriously hurt. I think he had one or two minor burns on his hands and that was all. Joy was playing the piano in the living room and he'd shouted at her to leave so she got out safely, too."

"The piano. I guess it's gone, too."

"Everything's gone. I'm so sorry, Ginny."

She began to cry. "Thanks for calling, Carla." She hung up and began to sob.

Ginny tried to explain to Leland but she was crying too hard to get the words out. It was as if the narrow thread that had connected her to the past, and to Ohio, had been irrevocably cut. Of course she hadn't planned to move back into the house ever. But knowing it was still there—and particularly her piano—had given her some feeling of continuity. Now it seemed it was gone forever.

ELEVEN

Ginny dragged through December, unable to feel the least Christmas spirit. The stores and streets were decorated—had been, of course, since Halloween—and the malls had their Santas ensconced on thrones or in gingerbread houses. But she wondered how anyone could possibly feel like Christmas when the temperature was in the eighties. She sent out obligatory Christmas cards, but her notes were much briefer than usual. She was unable to describe the year's events as she'd always done. She couldn't bear to relive these past months sixty-seven times, so she wrote a breezy sentence or two saying "Guess what? We're living in Florida now so I guess Santa will have to come by surfboard," and let it go at that.

The malls were so crowded she had to drive around the parking area several times waiting for a car to pull out before she could pull into a parking spot. And then she didn't know what to buy. She was looking at blouses one day for Susan when she was seized by a strange vertigo.

Surrounded by endless racks of clothes, she had a sense of drowning in a sea of blouses, skirts and dresses, as if a multi-colored tidal wave were bearing down on her. Ginny ran out into the center of the mall, her heart beating furiously. She took a few deep breaths trying to calm herself. When she finally regained her poise, she went directly home without buying a single present.

Leland was beginning to lose patience with her. He was

adjusting very nicely to his new style of living and went off happily each morning with his golf foursome. He could not understand why she didn't love Florida as much as he did.

"You look so grim," he would say. "This is supposed to be the season of joy. Why don't you show a little enthusiasm?"

At first she tried to tell him how disjointed she felt, how she couldn't seem to connect with anything down here. But he told her she wasn't trying hard enough to adjust. It was a matter of "mind set," he said. "You have to make up your mind you're going to like it, and then it will happen."

She tried over and over to think positive thoughts, but her mind wouldn't go along with the game. It had ideas of its own.

The one thing she was looking forward to was Susan and Donald's visit. They'd managed to take off a whole week and would be flying in on the 24th.

She and Leland bought a ceiling-high tree, and Ginny got out the decorations from under the guest bed the night before they were to arrive. Every year they'd added to the collection of ornaments, and it brought back a flood of memories as each was hung.

There was the baby in the half walnut shell that Melba had given her the year Donald was born. And the miniature auto reminded her of the year she and Leland were up all night putting together a pedal car for Donald. They'd been aghast when they opened the box to find dozens of small parts that had to be assembled. It took them till 4 A.M., and they were nearly hysterical from laughter and fatigue by the time they figured out how to do it. But Donald's excitement on Christmas morning made it all worthwhile. They could hardly get him out of it long enough to eat that day. It had snowed heavily on Christmas Eve so he was obliged to drive it in circles in the garage, but that didn't dampen his spirits in the least.

Leland had stored the car all those years in a corner of the basement, thinking he would pass it on to his grandchildren. But the grandchildren had yet to appear, and he reluctantly sold it at the yard sale.

The next afternoon they picked up Donald and Susan at the airport. Leland's first question was "How's the weather in Cleveland?" He seemed obsessed with weather now, and it was the first question he asked whenever he talked to out-of-state family or friends. The local TV stations encouraged this fixation with lengthy weather reports, and it seemed to Ginny they almost drooled over the miserable conditions elsewhere. Leland always got particularly excited when bad weather hit Columbus.

"Oh, those poor SOBs," he'd say gleefully. "I'll bet Rick Hoff is up to his ass shoveling show."

And so it was with obvious relish that he greeted Donald's answer of "Really lousy, Dad. The streets were so slick we called the taxi an hour early to make sure we would get to the airport on time."

"Well, son, we've had above average temperatures all month. You'll have to get yourselves a tan to impress them at the office." One would have thought he personally had arranged for the warmth and sunshine especially for their vacation.

When they arrived at the condo, Susan took Donald by the arm and led him into the living room. "Look at the view. Don't you just love this place?"

"How do you like it now that we've settled in?" Leland asked. Ginny had better sense than ask such a question of Susan.

"Very nice," she said with just a hint of hesitation. "Are you planning to recover that chair?" she asked Ginny, pointing to her old favorite in the flowered print.

"Absolutely not," she answered abruptly with no apologies. "Let's show Donald the rest of the condo."

Donald, befuddled as always by the women's exchange, followed them meekly to the kitchen. He "ohed" and "ahed" on cue and exclaimed appropriately over the rest of the rooms.

"It gets dark pretty early now," Ginny said. "Do you want to get in a lick at the beach while I get supper going?"

Leland went with them while Ginny cooked a festive dinner of shrimp and stone crab claws.

Later they went to the midnight services at Siesta Key chapel, an unlikely-looking church constructed on stilts, and hidden in a mass of jungle-like growth. The warm breezes that flowed through the sanctuary belied the sounds of carols as the voices of the congregation carried through the fragrant night. Ginny kept reminding herself that the Christ child was born on a night such as this but she still missed the festiveness of cold and snow at Christmastime in Ohio.

Ginny awoke early the next morning and prepared a sumptuous breakfast before waking the others.

"Come on, lazybones," she shook Leland's leg. "Breakfast is ready, and we can't lie about all Christmas Day."

Susan and Donald shuffled into the kitchen like zombies. They were still feeling a little jet-lagged.

"What's wrong with you guys?" Ginny asked. "Surely you must stay up late once in a while at home."

"It's the letdown, Mom." Donald rubbed his eyes and sipped his coffee. He looked so vulnerable with his hair uncombed, and creases from sleeping still marking his face, she could almost see the little boy in him again. So sweet and needy.

"Susan and I both work our tails off. Sometimes right through the weekend. As long as we keep going, it's okay. But once we stop, it really hits us, and we feel like we've been run over by a ten-ton truck. Don't expect us to be full of vim and vigor this week. We're going to be real flakes."

She patted his arm. "That's the idea. I didn't expect anything else." She wanted to add that she thought it was crazy to work themselves to death.

When they finished breakfast, they all gathered by the tree to exchange gifts, Ginny playing Santa and passing out the presents one by one. There were the usual things: stationery, cologne, fancy cheeses. She'd bought Brooks Brothers' shirts and ties for Donald, the only kind he would wear, and gave Susan a gift certificate from the choicest women's fashion store in Cleveland. She told her she hesitated to buy her anything because it might not fit, but the truth was their taste in clothes was so different she couldn't hope to suit Susan.

They, in turn, gave Ginny a leather handbag which looked very expensive, but now she would have to buy shoes to match.

Donald and Susan gave each other small token gifts since they planned to buy a High Definition TV when they got back home.

Ginny had chosen the finest rod and reel outfit she could find for Leland. He'd not done much fishing yet, having gone out once or twice with his old equipment and complaining it was inadequate. He seemed genuinely delighted with it.

"This is a beauty, Ginny," he exclaimed. "We're going to have to buy a small freezer since I'm going to be catching so many fish now." Ginny hadn't anticipated this and wondered where they could possibly put one.

Leland gave her a bestseller she'd been wanting to read for a while, and a very sexy, almost all-lace black nightgown. It was completely uncharacteristic of him as he invariably bought her practical things.

She was sure there was a message there. But was it: "I'm sorry as hell about the infidelity" or "I'd appreciate it if you'd act a little sexier"? She wasn't sure she wanted to find out. And it was a little embarrassing for her to open the nightgown in front of Donald and Susan even though they were all adults.

"Oh, look," Susan said as they were putting the torn up wrappings in a trash bag. "Here's an envelope on the tree addressed to you, Ginny."

She'd forgotten the envelope that had been in the box of gifts that Melba had sent them. She'd stuck it on a tree branch for fear it would get accidently thrown away.

She tore it open. It was an open-dated plane ticket round-trip to Columbus. With it was a note.

When you can't stand the heat, come up and visit me. Love, Melba.

Bless Melba. If anyone was intuitive, it was her sister. This made Christmas Day almost endurable.

TWELVE

Donald and Susan were true to their word about wanting to do nothing but lie about on the beach and vegetate for a week. They weren't even particularly anxious to go out to eat, perfectly content to let Ginny prepare their meals for them. Ginny tried to feel put upon, but truthfully she didn't want to wait in long lines at the restaurants, and she enjoyed being able to impress them with her culinary skills. Leland took her cooking for granted, so she went all out when company came.

Occasionally she would sit with them on the beach, but all they wanted to talk about was their work, and that soon wore thin on her.

Several evenings they played bridge, but the others took it so seriously, and played so competitively, that Ginny didn't enjoy it. She was used to playing with a group of women in Columbus who were more interested in gossip than Goren. She really needed to find a group like that here.

"For heaven's sake, bid," Leland growled the first night, as Ginny sat engrossed in watching a brightly lit sightseeing boat not far from shore. They had looped red and green Christmas lights around the regular white ones, and it looked like a slowly moving Christmas tree on the smooth waters of the Gulf.

Her attention wandered so much that she and Susan were three hundred and fifty points behind the men.

"Why don't we switch partners tomorrow?" Susan said, smiling archly at Ginny. "We should try different combinations each night. How about you and Donald playing together tomorrow, Ginny?"

She couldn't feel insulted because she knew how poorly she'd played.

The next day while everyone else was on the beach, Ginny studied her rule book, concentrating particularly on the bidding guidelines, her weakest point. When the game started that evening, she sat there grim and resolute, vowing not to say a word except to bid. But each hand seemed worse than the one before, and in spite of her unflagging attention and determination to show she could play well, it seemed hopeless. In the end Leland and Susan overwhelmed them.

"You can't help it if you have lousy cards, Mom," Donald said afterward. But she could tell he was disappointed they did so poorly. He had a habit of going over the bidding of the last hand and telling her how she "might have" (she knew he meant "should have") played it differently.

Ordinarily Ginny did not mind losing. In their club, the hostess provided a silly gift to the winner, but it was just for laughs. But this time the three of them had turned this entertaining pastime into some kind of a battle of wits. Or was it guts? Did young people have to be so competitive over everything? So what was Leland's excuse?

She didn't want to play any more, but they insisted they had to finish out the rotation the next night. She couldn't act like a spoiled child by refusing to do it.

"Okay, kid," Leland said as he dealt the cards for the final round, "we're going to beat the heck out of them tonight. No dreaming, no gazing out the window, just total concentration."

"I didn't take my eyes off this card table last night," she answered. "I couldn't help it if I got nothing but lousy hands."

"Well, I've got the cards stacked tonight, so there are no excuses."

Ginny was so nervous she could feel perspiration trickle down her back. She knew it was absurd to be so uptight over a game, but Leland was making this into serious competition. For once, though, she got some fairly good hands, and she felt as though she played them well. She even bid and made a small slam, something she rarely had the courage to attempt. But while she and Leland had good cards, Susan and Donald had some sensational ones, and in the end it was Susan and Donald who won by several hundred points.

"We sure bombed on that one," Leland said sulkily.

"It was just the way the cards fell," Donald said waving his hand above the cards scattered on the table. "Our hands happened to mesh beautifully tonight."

"I think if some different ones had been led . . ." Leland's voice drifted off but it was clear that he didn't feel responsible.

"No way," Donald was insistent. "Mom played really well tonight, the best I've ever seen her. It's just that we had better cards than you did."

"Well, maybe . . ." Leland wasn't going to accept the defeat gracefully or give her any credit for trying her best. Donald was sweet for his compliment, but she wanted to *wring* Leland's neck.

Susan had been silent until now, looking a little smug over their victory. "I was really amazed at how well you played tonight, Ginny. Truly, if you'd had a few better cards, you two probably would have won."

Ginny was amused. It was one of Susan's typical backhanded compliments, but somehow it ended the evening on the right note.

The next day was the last full day that Susan and Donald would be with them. They were flying back early New Year's Eve to attend a party given by Susan's firm.

"I want to spend the whole day on the beach," Susan said at the breakfast table. "I intend to soak up every last ray of sunshine I can. When we go to that party tomorrow night, they're all going to drop dead when they see my tan."

Susan had the kind of skin that turned a beautiful bronze in a very short time. With her black hair and large brown eyes, she was a very attractive young woman. But when she was as tan as she'd gotten this week, she turned heads. And she knew it.

"According to the weatherman, you're going to be blessed with one of Florida's finest today." Leland poured coffee all around. "I ordered it up especially for you."

Ginny hadn't gone out with them much. Her fair complexion left her vulnerable to burning. She was alarmed at the wrinkles beginning to appear at the corner of her eyes and the little ridges around her lips. She always did her shelling first thing in the morning, and she wore sun screen and sheltered her face with a large-brimmed hat.

But today she wanted to be with them though, because God knew when she would see them again. She was infinitely grateful they'd spent a whole week there although she was sure the lure of the beach was probably responsible. But that was all right as long as *she* got to see them.

Siesta beach in front of their building was chock-a-block with holiday visitors, their brilliantly colored beach towels spread haphazardly over the fine white sand like a mammoth collage. Ginny thought it would be a wonderful sight to float over the beach in a hot air balloon, viewing the scene as if it were an abstract painting, a Lichtenstein canvas perhaps, but instead of lines and dabs of paint, there would be blotches of beach towels and dashes of reclining bodies. But she didn't share her thoughts.

As the four of them spread out their towels, Ginny said, "I need some exercise. I've eaten too much this week. Think I'll walk down to Point of Rocks and back. Any takers?"

"I'll pass. This is my last chance to be a total slouch." Susan stretched out on her towel and began to read a book.

"I'll keep Susan company," said Leland. "Why don't you two go on." Although he could be blindly insensitive at times, Ginny realized that Leland understood she wanted to have a little time alone with Donald. They so rarely had the chance to be together without others around.

They started out for the south end of the beach that ended in an area of jutting rocks, their tops worn smooth by waves over the centuries. Everyone was stripped to the basics here. She'd learned that it was just as likely to be a rich and powerful executive dressed in the ragged shorts and battered cap as not. The beach was the great leveler, putting everyone at the same disadvantage of having to display all the defects and imperfections of their bodies. Of course the young ones with their beautiful aerobically-fit bodies loved the opportunity to show it all off. And did they ever flaunt it. But each decade of life added to or took away something, and the bathing suits covered more and more accordingly.

She'd noted with interest, however, that at a certain point in life, people didn't give a damn any more. It was as if they came to the realization that their body was old and unattractive and so what? They were no longer self conscious about it. Ginny wished she could achieve that mind set.

It was the babies and children, however, that fascinated her the most. She couldn't take her eyes off the toddlers as they approached the water. Some were terrified of the small waves that lapped harmlessly at their feet. No amount of encouragement from their parents would calm them, and they would scream until carried far away from the threatening Gulf. Others would take to the sea as if they were born to it, refusing to leave when it was time to go. There was something so refreshing about children and their unequivocal likes and dislikes. No subtle double meanings; no beating around the bush.

She pointed one out to Donald. The child seemed totally fearless in the water. "That's the way you were," she said. "We thought you were going to drown yourself."

"I've loved the seashore ever since I can remember," he said.

The older children were fun to watch, too. Many of them were building sand castles, and they would become so intent on their construction that they seemed unaware of the crowds of beach goers who flowed around them. They would build delightfully whimsical structures, their creativity not yet curtailed by disapproving adults.

Donald had been walking silently beside her for quite a while so she guessed she would have to initiate any further conversation.

"We've hardly had a chance to talk this week," she said. "Tell me how your job is going."

"It's high pressure stuff, but you know me, Mom. The busier, the better. We've got a big shopping center well along in the planning stages, and we'll break ground this spring. I told Dad but I don't know if he told you that I expect a promotion soon."

"That's great, hon. And what about Susan's job? She seems so enthusiastic; that's not an act is it?"

"Oh, no, she eats it up. You know she's really got her eye on a partnership. That can't happen for a couple more years, but I think she's got a good chance."

Ginny had always vowed not to interfere in their lives in any way. She detested meddling mother-in-laws, her own had done a fair amount of it before she had a stroke and ended up in a nursing home, but she couldn't help but say in what she hoped was a joshing tone, "I hope you two aren't burnt out by the time you're forty."

"Don't worry about us. We thrive on it. As much as we've

enjoyed this week off, we're both getting antsy to get back to work."

"I guess I should be thankful I got to see you at all." It sounded more whiny than she intended.

"We'll be back," he said. "Don't you worry."

They walked on in silence. Just ahead a young couple carried identical twin toddlers to the edge of the water. The children were beautiful with tight auburn curls and bright blue eyes, and they were attracting a lot of attention. Both babies seemed to love the water, and plopped themselves down at the waterline to splash and giggle.

Ginny was entranced.

"Look at those adorable babies," she said, grabbing Donald's arm to guide him toward them. "I don't know when I've seen anything so cute."

"You seem to dwell on babies a lot," he answered.

"What are you talking about?"

"You always bring up the subject around us."

"It's just a natural part of my conversation." She stopped short and looked up at him. "What on earth are you trying to say, Donald?"

"I'm saying that ever since we've been married, you've continually talked about babies, and it strikes us that these are very broad hints."

She couldn't believe him. She never consciously had done so. "You know I'd never do that. You're supersensitive."

"Maybe so. But I might as well put my cards on the table, Mom. Susan and I have decided not to have children. She's put too much time and effort into her career, and she wants to concentrate on that. Besides, we don't think the world is such a great place to bring up kids."

"Oh." Ginny was surprised. She didn't have any idea they felt this way.

"Is that all you have to say?" he asked.

"What the *hell* else is there to say?" She rarely swore, but this just came out involuntarily.

"Mom!"

"Look, it's your life and your business, and I don't intend to discuss it further."

"That's fine with me."

The day suddenly seemed less bright, and she tried not to look at any of the children on the beach; it made her too sad. But she didn't want their visit to end this way.

Just before they returned to Susan and Leland, she said to Donald, "I'm sorry I lost my cool. You two have every right to decide not to have kids. You can't have a baby just because your mother wants to be a grandma." Which, she now realized, she did want more than she'd ever been conscious of.

"I'm sorry, Mom. I can understand how you feel, but I think it's the right decision for us. Thanks for being a good sport."

She tried her best to smile. "That's your mom. World's Champion Good Sport."

Donald gave her a hug, and she hung onto him for an extra moment, not wanting to let him go. "I love you, Mom," he said in her ear.

"Love you, too," she answered.

Thirteen

After the first of the year, the visits began. When they left Columbus they'd said, "Come see us." They didn't realize that everyone would take them at their word. Ginny began to feel like a hired maid and cook, but in spite of the extra work the visits involved, she enjoyed them. It kept her occupied, gave her little time to think, and that suited her fine.

First came Leland's nephew, his wife, and baby for several days the second week in January. Ginny thought the seven-month-old baby girl, poor thing, was one of the homeliest children she'd ever seen. But the parents thought otherwise and made over the child as if she were beautiful. "How's my pretty one," or "You're my little doll baby" was the way they addressed her, and after hearing them talk to her that way throughout the visit, Ginny began to think the baby was rather cute after all.

"I've been brainwashed," she told Leland in private. "The longer they're here, the cuter Cheryl looks to me."

"All babies look cute to you, Ginny." He peered at her over his newspaper.

"True. But I think it's because they're absolutely crazy about her that's so endearing."

"They waited eight years to have her. Linda couldn't get pregnant and went through all kinds of tests and surgery. So it's not surprising."

"Oh, I had no idea." How strange the world was when those who desperately wanted children often couldn't have them, or had to go through hell to conceive, and those who probably could get pregnant the minute they tried sometimes didn't want them.

After they left, it was only a week before Ginny's brother Wally and his wife Constance arrived from Mansfield, Ohio.

"Hey, by golly, this is really something!" Wally boomed as Leland opened the door. Their plane had been delayed by a snowstorm in Ohio, so they were nearly two hours late. They'd picked up a rental car at the airport in case the women wanted to go off on their own.

"Oh, this is really nice," Connie said in her soft voice. "You two are so lucky to be able to live here."

"That's what I keep telling Ginny." Leland gave her a sidelong glance.

The next morning Wally declined an invitation to play golf. "My belly gets in the way of my swing," he laughed, but he agreed to go out on a fishing boat with Leland for the day.

That left Ginny to entertain Constance, and that seemed a formidable task. She was very quiet and self effacing, preferring to stay in the background as Wally always dominated the conversation. Ginny felt as if she barely knew Constance although they'd been sisters-in-law for over thirty years.

"Well, what shall we do today?" she asked after the men had left. "Do you want to shop or go to a movie? Or would you like to spend the day on the beach?"

"Would you mind taking me to someone's house?"

"Oh, do you have a friend here?" Ginny asked, surprised.

"I haven't actually met her, but I've corresponded with her. She said if I was ever in town to be sure and look her up."

"That would be fine. Why don't you give her a call and see if she's home." Ginny was delighted at the thought of having a third person around. She wasn't sure she could sustain a lengthy conversation with Constance. They'd had little opportunity over the years to find any common ground, and she simply didn't know what to talk about with her. She loved her brother dearly, but in his garrulousness, he so overwhelmed Constance that she seemed almost devoid of personality.

Her friend was not only home but invited them to visit her that afternoon. Constance told Ginny about her during the drive to Casey Key where she lived.

"Her name is Naomi Catalano, and she's a poet. I'd read several of her books of poetry and was so impressed I wrote her through her publisher. She was nice enough to answer me, and we've kept on corresponding. I've sent her some of my own poetry for comment, and she's been very helpful."

"Your poetry! I had no idea you wrote poems, Constance."

"Oh, yes, I've written them for years, but I've only gotten up my nerve recently to try and get them published. I've had three accepted by literary magazines this year."

"That's terrific. Why haven't you ever said anything about it?"

"The opportunity just never came up to mention it, I guess. Wally kids me about it so I'm not anxious to talk about it in front of him. He says I'm a freelance writer all right because I give it all away for free. Of course those magazines don't pay you anything, but I feel it's quite an honor to get in them."

"I would think so. I hope you'll let me read them."

Constance actually blushed when Ginny glanced at her. "I brought some with me to show my friend."

Apparently there was more to Constance than Ginny had ever dreamed.

Casey Key was directly south of Siesta Key, but the two islands were not connected. They had to drive down Tamiami Trail, Route 41, to get there. Ginny loved Casey Key. There were no high rises there, only an odd mixture of fabulously expensive homes and modest ones. Prices had been escalating rapidly on the island, and the older homes were being remodeled and added on to or else torn down to make way for huge new ones.

The island was so narrow that every home had a bay or gulf view. Thousands of palm trees interspersed with sea grape gave it an exotic flavor.

Naomi's home was a small cypress house nearly hidden by bougainvillea and overgrown hibiscus bushes. It was on the bay side of the island and a long screened porch looked out over the Intracoastal Waterway. The overstuffed furniture, placed haphazardly around the living room, looked very comfortable but worn, and it was obvious she had settled here long before Casey Key real estate had become one of the hottest items on the local market. Ginny felt at home immediately.

Naomi greeted them warmly. She was dressed in blue jeans and a faded and stretched tee shirt, her graying hair worn long and straight, held back from her face by a tortoise shell headband. Although Ginny usually thought long hair was unbecoming to older women, somehow it seemed appropriate to Naomi's square, rather masculine features. She was a striking, if not a beautiful, woman. There were several large, showy rings on her fingers. Ginny judged she and Naomi were close to the same age.

"I'm so delighted to finally get to meet you, Constance," she said. "It's always fun to try and figure out what people are like from reading their poetry and then see if your concept of them holds up. I've always thought of you as one of those quiet souls who run deep. Am I right?" she asked Ginny.

"I think you've got it," she grinned, and saw Constance blush deeply. "I've been her sister-in-law for years and just discovered that she wrote poetry."

"That figures. Suits my image of her to a T. Well, let's not embarrass Constance any more. Let's go sit on the porch."

A soft breeze rustled the palm fronds and the three women sat in the cool shadows of the porch. Constance had brought some poems along to discuss with Naomi. Ginny was impressed with their beautiful images and the subtle emotions the poems evoked. This was truly a facet she had never suspected in her sister-in-law.

"Do you do any writing?" Naomi asked her when they had finished.

"I did as a teenager. I used to wake up in the middle of the night thinking of a poem and couldn't go back to sleep until I'd written it down. Then I guess I just lost interest after that. It seemed to me that so much of the new poetry was unintelligible. I didn't want to do that sort of thing."

"Naomi, would you mind reading some of your poems for Ginny?" Constance asked. "I think you'll see that not all poetry has to be obscure. You'll love it."

"Sure, I'm all ham. Let me go get some."

When she went in the house, Constance said, "Isn't she marvelous? I like her even more than I thought I would."

"She certainly is a character. I'm really glad you brought me down here, Constance."

Naomi emerged from the house carrying several thin books of poetry, and a tray with a carafe of coffee, three cups, and cream and sugar. There were also some hand-rolled cigarettes.

"Either of you want some grass? I find I appreciate my poetry better when I'm a little high," she laughed.

Ginny and Constance looked at each other trying not to register shock or disapproval. They both murmured no thanks as if they were offered pot all the time.

Naomi poured the coffee, lit up, and settled back into her chair with one of her books. Ginny was feeling slightly uncomfortable now, not knowing what to expect.

Naomi began to read in a soft, singsong voice, pronouncing

the words slowly and emphasizing syllables that gave her reading a lilt.

Ginny relaxed, and let the words wash over her as she watched the moving shadows on the porch ceiling made by the waving palm fronds. Soon she was caught up in the music of the poetry, awed by the images it evoked for her, lulled by the flow. Constance was right. Her poetry was neither obscure, nor rambling. It was succinct, metaphorical and poignant. If she had known poetry could be like this, she would have read it all along, but instead she had shunned it for years thinking she'd never understand it.

It was as if she was being drawn into another world full of eloquence and beauty, though this other world was often sad.

"This poem is called 'Transference,' " Naomi said and proceeded to read:

> *The mockingbird*
> *held captive in the sweet gum tree*
> *pours out his great*
> *encumbrance of song*
> *unmindful of my need for sleep.*
> *He must disburse*
> *the night's supply*
> *of twitterings and trills,*
> *so weighty that*
> *he sits immobilized*
> *till every note*
> *has been released*
> *and he can fly again.*
> *And as this rogue*
> *is being drained of melody,*
> *each phrase, so pure and clear,*
> *floats up and fills my empty heart.*

Ginny didn't know what happened to her, but suddenly she felt herself sobbing uncontrollably, having difficulty catching her breath. She was so startled at herself, she felt like an utter fool, but she couldn't seem to stop the tears.

Naomi got up and put her arm around her shoulder. "I must have hit a nerve. Sorry."

Ginny fumbled in her purse for a hankie. She dabbed at her eyes and began to laugh self consciously. "Good heavens, I'm not normally the sentimental type. I don't know why it hit me like that."

"Sometimes," Naomi said sitting down again, "there are feelings deep inside us that we are unaware of. Poetry has a way of calling up these feelings for better or worse. I guess this is a good time to call an end to our reading."

"It was beautiful," Ginny said. "I-um-don't need to tell you how much it touched me."

"Why don't you consider writing some poetry again?" Naomi cajoled. "Obviously there are a lot of emotions there you could draw on. The older we get, the more we have stored away bits and pieces of feelings and experiences that we can write about. Let's face it, we've all been through a lot, and writing is just one way to try and make some sense of it."

"Oh, I don't know. It's been so many years I probably don't have the knack any more. It seems too late to start in again."

"Believe me, it is never too late."

"Really, Ginny," Constance said, "you ought to give it a try. You don't ever have to show it to anyone else. But it's terrific therapy."

Ginny put her handkerchief away and smiled. "The therapy part I think I could use."

They said their goodbyes to Naomi who urged Ginny again to try her hand at poetry. "My number's in the phone book. Please give me a call or come down any time. Bring some of your writing along or else we'll just chat."

"I'll do that," she answered, more to be polite than out of any conviction she would follow their advice.

They rode much of the way home in silence while Ginny tried to sort out her emotions, attempting to understand why she had reacted so strongly to that poem. She supposed the phrase "empty heart" had triggered the tears. There had been a number of times these past months that her heart had felt very empty indeed.

FOURTEEN

With genuine sadness she kissed Constance goodbye at the end of the week. She'd gained new respect for her sister-in-law as Ginny realized she was not the dull, unimaginative person she'd thought her to be. It was quite a shock to learn she had so completely misunderstood her all these years.

"I hope you two come back often," she told them.

"Hey," Wally said gripping her in a bear hug, "with a place like this, you're going to have trouble keeping us away." He put his arm around Constance's shoulder. "Isn't that right, kid?"

"I enjoyed every minute," she said, "and, Ginny, I hope you'll give your writing a try."

After they left, Leland flopped into a chair. "That brother of yours wears me out. For all his weight, he sure goes strong. That man has the constitution of an ox."

"That's what they always said about Dad until he dropped dead of a heart attack at fifty-eight."

Changing the subject, Leland never liked to talk about death and dying, he asked, "What was that business about writing that Constance said to you?"

"Oh, you know, I told you we visited that friend of hers on Casey Key. I didn't say anything while they were here because Wally teases her, but she's been writing poetry. And Naomi has been corresponding with her and giving her suggestions. They both were trying to get me interested in trying my hand."

"Poetry, huh? You mean like 'roses are red . . . ?' Are you seriously going to do that?"

Ginny wished that Constance had not brought up the subject. She had a feeling that Leland would be no more enlightened than Wally.

"Oh, maybe. Who knows?" She really didn't plan to, but now she was curious to hear what Leland would say.

"Can you make money at it?"

"I don't think so, Leland. Constance has had a few published, but she said they didn't pay her anything."

"Well, that's pretty dumb to give it away free. If she's smart, she'd do advertising copy if she's so hot on writing. That's were the money is."

"Oh come on, Leland, is it always the bottom line that counts?"

He squirmed more firmly into the chair seat and did a silent drum roll on the arms with his fingers. "That's the name of the game, isn't it? What if I'd been out there selling for nothing? You'd have gotten pretty damn hungry, dear."

It took a minute for Ginny to be able to answer him calmly. Finally she said in a voice as even as she could make it, "I don't think it's the same thing, Leland." Then she went into the kitchen to make supper.

The other units were fully occupied now. Next door on the right were the Greenwalds from New Jersey. Joseph Greenwald had suffered a stroke the year before and was confined to a wheelchair. His wife, Maria, was a frail ethereal creature who devoted every minute to her husband's comfort, and she would not leave him alone for even short periods. Ginny couldn't conceive what it would be like to be a prisoner in your home the way Maria was. She wondered why they bothered to come to Florida since they never ventured out. She even had someone deliver the groceries to her.

On the other side of them the LaClercs came from Montreal. Instead of being housebound like the Greenwalds, they were gone much of the time. They loved to gamble, and if they weren't at the dog races in town, they were in Tampa at the jai alai games. Most evenings they could find a bingo game to satisfy their compulsion for games of chance.

Ginny had hoped she could find someone whom she could call on now and then for shopping, lunch or a movie, but there seemed no one around who could fill that role.

She was glad when their former neighbors, the Hoffs, came for a visit two weeks after Constance and Wally had left.

"Tell me about the house," Ginny said to Carla almost as soon as they'd exchanged hellos.

"Not much has happened yet. I guess there is some problem with the insurance. What they hope to do is tear it down and build something brand new."

"It can't be saved at all?"

"There was too much damage," Carla said. "I'll tell you, it's depressing to look at it day after day. I can't wait till they tear it down. It really gets to me."

"What about Joy and Dave? Where are they staying?"

"They're in a small apartment down by campus. Joy's pregnant so they're anxious to get the house built."

"Oh, that's wonderful. I'm so happy for her." She thought that Carla probably did not know about the baby Joy lost, and she was not going to mention it. She prayed that this time it would work out for her.

Leland was delighted that Gordon wanted to golf, so the men were on the golf course during most of their visit. Carla was mainly interested in the beach which was an easy, relaxing way to entertain.

When it came time for the Hoffs to return to Columbus, both had acquired deep tans and Carla had the inevitable bag

of shells to take home with her.

That night, Ginny lay in bed wide awake. "Do you know what Carla said about this place?" she asked Leland.

"What?"

"She said how quiet and peaceful it is."

Leland laid his book down on his stomach with a sigh. "I know it's quiet and peaceful. Is something wrong with that?"

"And she wasn't the only one to say it. Everybody says it."

"Get to the point, Ginny. I know you're not interrupting my reading to tell me how right I've been all along."

Touché. She knew she'd started venting her frustrations at night in bed. It's just that things seemed to build up in her throughout the day, and by bedtime they were fermenting so much in her mind that it was impossible to go to sleep until she unloaded them. And she'd decided the day she met Naomi that she couldn't keep everything bottled up inside her anymore.

"It's too quiet. That's what's wrong with it. It took me a while to figure it out, but I'm certain that's it."

"You're not making sense. How can a place be *too* quiet?" Leland asked, annoyed now at her statement.

"It's not normal. A neighborhood should have kids around and people of all ages. It should be full of life, not death. Do you know that two residents in this condo died this month? It was in the newsletter. This place is a waiting room for the hereafter."

"Oh, come on. You're exaggerating."

"I'm not, Leland. I want to move out of here into an area where there are young people. I want to be able to see some kids once in a while. I feel a million years old."

Leland sat up straighter in bed, letting his book slip unnoticed to the floor. She could tell how agitated he was by the way he gripped the edge of the covers.

"Here we are in this beautiful condominium, the envy of all

our friends and relatives, and you want to move out! I'll tell you, Ginny, I have no intention of moving. Frankly, I think you're still sore about not having grandkids. You're just going to have to accept that and get on with your life. Give it some time; you'll get over it." His anger seemed to have worked itself out, and he ended on almost an apologetic note.

He was probably right. She was overreacting to Donald's revelation. She only knew she was acutely unhappy. But Leland, who had never been especially intuitive about her emotional needs, seemed even less sensitive lately. Did he think she simply was being hysterical, and that stonewalling was the best defense?

Now that he was retired, he could dig in and have it his way twenty-four hours a day if he wished. Whatever the case, it was obvious that he was implacable, and whatever she was going to do about her discontent, she would have to do without his help.

"I'm trying to, Leland. I'm really trying to adapt," she said although she wondered how much longer it would take her to do so.

FIFTEEN

"When are you coming down?" Ginny had called Melba in desperation. All the company had come and gone, and they were alone again. Leland was now playing golf every morning and fishing in the afternoons, and Ginny didn't know what to do with herself. Even the shelling was beginning to lose its appeal. She'd run out of places to store the bags of shells, and she could never figure out what to do with them anyway. At times she was tempted to dump them back on the beach for someone else to discover, but she'd given up so much lately she couldn't quite make herself part with the one thing she enjoyed about being stuck in Florida.

"Hadn't planned on coming. You know how Mickey hates the kennels, and I have nowhere else to leave him. Why don't you use the ticket I sent you and come see me?"

"Not now, Melba. For one thing I couldn't bear to see our house. Carla tells me they're held up by the insurance settlement, and it's still sitting there. I'm depressed enough without seeing that."

"Well, you don't have to go over there you know."

"I'm afraid I'd have a compulsion to see it, even though it would break my heart. That sounds silly, I suppose, but I just want to stay away from Columbus till it's torn down."

"What's wrong, Ginny? You sound so sad, and I thought you'd be happy down there."

"I don't know, Melba. I just can't seem to get my act together.

Leland's happy as a clam, but I'm just floundering around trying to find my niche. I miss all my friends. And it seems so strange having no one but old people living around you."

"Then find some way to get involved with children."

"How?"

"I haven't the faintest idea, dear. That's something you'll have to figure out. And if you change your mind about coming up, let me know."

"I will, Melba."

Ginny began to take a folding chair and some magazines to the beach in the afternoons because by two or two-thirty when school was out, the children would appear. It was a refreshing change from the condo pool where the residents congregated. She'd joined them once or twice, but she tired quickly of the conversations that centered on soap operas, illnesses, and operations. It was far more interesting and cheering to watch the toddlers play in the surf or the older youngsters build sand castles.

At first she tried to read, but she found her interest was caught more and more by the children at play. One day she took some kitchen utensils with her to try her hand at making a sand castle, in hopes that some children might join her.

She filled her scrub bucket with empty cans, cookie cutters, a bread pan and a pie server. At the beach she found an unoccupied expanse of sand where she dropped her flip flops and utensils. Filling her bucket in the surf, she wet the fine sand just enough to make it the consistency of workable clay and began to fashion a castle.

A young girl about six wearing a scarlet suit pulled her mother toward Ginny's sculpture. "Look, Mommy, I want to make one like that. Can we get some pans so I can do it, too?"

"Why don't you help me?" Ginny smiled at the child, holding out the pie server to her. "I really could use a good helper."

"You wouldn't mind?" asked the mother.

"Of course not. I'd love it." She turned to the child. "Hi, I'm Ginny," she said. "And what's your name?"

"Amanda."

"Let's see how well you can smooth that wall there," Ginny said as she pointed to the north side of the structure.

The girl sat down happily on the far side of the castle, and Ginny passed her some of her containers.

Soon the child was blissfully engrossed in making a tower by using a soup can for a mold for the battlements. Her mother lay on a beach towel nearby cheering her on.

A little while later two little boys came by. "Hey, lady," said the bigger one, a skinny kid whose peeling arms and back looked like the fraying edges of hot pink tissue paper. "That's cool. We're pretty good at that stuff, too. Dontcha need us to make some great big towers?" He held his hand over his head to indicate the height of the proposed additions.

Ginny gestured for them to join in. "We sure do. Let's see how tall you can make them."

It wasn't long before there were seven or eight children working on it. The castle grew rapidly with wings and towers jutting out in every direction like the masterpiece of an unrestrained and giddy architect. In addition to using Ginny's kitchen utensils, the children made tools from the most unlikely items: pen shells, the long, flat shells of smoky mother-of-pearl made exotic diggers; sun screen bottles were used for tamping the walls and towers; the eyepieces of sunglasses served for carving and poking holes. Some even used their flip flops as planes to smooth walkways and parapets.

The boys concentrated on building the tallest and straightest tower they could manage. The girls, more intent on decoration, collected colorful scallop shells in shades from beige to bright orange and arranged them in patterns on the walls till the ornamentation reminded Ginny of the intricate marble design on the cathedral Santa Maria del Fiore in Florence. They'd created a grand and imposing structure, and she felt a sense of pride as passersby were drawn to admire it. Of course the children deserved most of the credit for the sand castle, but she'd been the catalyst. She thought it must be the way it feels to conduct an orchestra, pulling together all the diverse talents to create a single beautiful melody.

After a couple of hours, Ginny glanced at her watch and realized it was time to get supper. She announced reluctantly, "Kids, I'm sorry, but I've got to go. Would you all please put your cups and tools in the bucket over here."

"Can we do it again tomorrow?" asked a round-faced little girl. "This is the mostest fun."

"Yeah, us too," said the boy with the peeling arms who had worked steadily all afternoon.

"Well, sure, if you'd like," Ginny said, as pleased as if she'd just been asked to run for public office.

The next day Ginny was there as promised and to her surprise almost every child from the day before showed up again. She decided she was on to something.

And so began her afternoon ritual. Every day at three-thirty that week she was on the beach with her pail full of utensils, and the children were there waiting when she arrived. Each day another child or two joined them, and there was an unspoken challenge to build a more elaborate castle than the day before. The children's capacity for inventiveness was unlimited.

At the end of the week, Leland asked her at dinner what she'd been doing with herself. It was his customary question; she was sure he didn't much care.

"I've been on the beach a lot," she replied. She wouldn't say more. She simply rose and cleared away the dishes instead.

The following Thursday, Ginny was intent on building a

particularly tall turret and was surrounded by a dozen or so children when she heard someone addressing her. She turned and saw a man with a camera slung around his neck.

"Excuse me. I'm from the *Herald-Tribune*. Someone called the editor and told us about the lady who builds sand castles. Would you mind if I ask you a few questions and take your picture?"

"What do you want to know?"

"How long have you been doing this?"

"Oh, a couple of weeks I guess." Ginny hadn't really counted the days. She just knew how much she looked forward to each one.

"Do you have a background in art or sculpture?"

She laughed. "Heavens no. It's just a fun thing anyone can do. You don't have to be an artist."

"What got you started doing this?"

She told him how she began to build a castle one day on a whim and how it had attracted some children. They all seemed to enjoy it so much that it had become an afternoon routine.

"And what do you get out of this?" the reporter asked her.

She reflected on his question for a moment. Then she turned and gave the nearest child a hug. "More than you'd realize. These kids have such a contagious spirit. Working with them makes me feel young again. This may not be the Fountain of Youth, but it's a darn good substitute."

He thanked her and took a number of pictures of her and the children at work on the castle. She felt embarrassed at the attention it generated among the beach goers, and she half hoped the pictures wouldn't come out and the article would be scrapped.

But it wasn't. The picture appeared in color on the front page of the local section in the next morning's edition. Underneath in bold letters it was captioned, "Sand Castle Lady."

She pointed it out to Leland, figuring that a direct approach was better than letting him discover it.

"Guess who?" she said lightly, unsure how he would react.

He studied it for a minute before realization dawned. "Well, that's dignified. My sixty-year-old wife playing in the sand. I suppose I'll get razzed unmercifully by my golf buddies."

That did it. She had felt a little foolish when she saw the picture, though it did please her to see the bright faces of the children who surrounded her. But Leland's statement made her furious. She began to say, "I suppose hitting a little ball around is so mature . . ."

But he wasn't listening. He was grumbling, "Sand castles, for Pete's sake."

Sixteen

Ginny continued to build sand castles every weekday afternoon and soon acquired some notoriety on the beach. Many people recognized and spoke to her, having seen her picture in the paper, and even more children congregated to help with the building. Some of their creations were so unique and such fun to do, she hated to see them destroyed; but if the tide or rain or later beach goers didn't level it, the kids would do so themselves before proceeding with a new castle. They couldn't very well fill up the entire beach with end-to-end castles, so they continued to rebuild on the same spot.

The subject was never discussed at home, however. She continued with her beach sculpture longer than she'd intended, egged on in part by Leland's attitude. She might have tired of it after a short while, but his put-down had challenged her, and the accumulation of frustrations made her determined to stand up against any disparagement. She was rather surprised at herself. She'd always considered herself easygoing, inclined to go-with-the-flow of things. But all that had happened these past few months had made her more feisty, less willing to give in or even compromise. She, belatedly, was turning into something of a fighter. One afternoon while she was on the beach, a young man in a business suit approached her. "Mrs. McAllister?"

She stood up, brushing sand from her legs. "Yes. Can I help you?" He looked rather ludicrous in his jacket and tie among all the scantily clad bathers.

"I'm Bud Greenwood from the Chamber of Commerce. I saw your picture in the paper, and I was wondering if you might like to serve as a judge in our annual sand sculpture contest. We hold it every March at the public beach, and we get lots of participants. I guess that's because we give out pretty good cash prizes," he said, stepping back to make room for a little boy carrying a bucket of water from the surf to the castle under construction.

"I'm no artist you know. I just do this for the fun of it. I don't know how good a judge I'd be." Ginny hesitated.

"We know you don't have formal training. There will be other judges who do. But you've made something of a name for yourself on the beach, and everyone associates you with sand castles. I think you'd make a nice addition to our judges' committee."

"Well, sure. It does sound like it would be fun."

"The contest will be on March tenth starting at ten. We're asking the judges to meet at the pavilion at nine to go over the rules and regulations together. We'll look forward to seeing you then."

"Thanks for asking me."

She was elated. It was such a simple thing, but somehow it validated her.

That evening at dinner she decided to tell Leland. She braced herself for his reaction, though she was determined not to let him get to her.

While they were eating dessert she said, "Leland, I've been asked to be a judge at the annual sand sculpture contest at the public beach."

"That's nice," he said blandly without lifting his eyes from his plate. He asked no questions and, in fact, changed the subject to talk about repair work on Route 41.

She was prepared for derision, but she wasn't ready for

complete indifference.

They didn't seem to connect any more. He had his fishing and golf that kept him busy all day, and she had—sand castles. It was a long way from being enough to fill her life, but at least it was something. For now it gave her a reason to get up in the morning and would keep her going, she hoped, until she could find something more meaningful.

She missed her friends dreadfully, the ones she shopped and lunched with, her bridge group, and most of all Melba. There wasn't anyone at Tranquility Gardens in whom she could confide, and it seemed that she and Leland had less and less to say to each other. There was always the surface talk—the weather, the traffic, the state of the economy. But he didn't want to listen to her worries and fears any more.

She had thought about volunteering at the hospital, but she became so depressed around sick people that she knew she couldn't do it in her present state of mind. They would have to cheer her up instead of the other way around.

She had inquired at the library about helping out, but there seemed to be dozens of professional librarians who were retired and anxious to fill up their time. There was little for someone untrained to do. Ginny felt utterly useless.

For the next two weeks she was more exacting when she worked with the children on the castles. She insisted on more symmetry, on smoother walls and parapets, on straighter towers. She looked forward to the sand sculpture contest. She was very flattered to have been asked, and it seemed like a good way to meet new people. She told the children about it and encouraged them all to participate. They weren't all equally talented, but she knew they'd all have fun participating in it.

On the tenth of March she walked to Siesta Public Beach which was only a few blocks from Tranquility Gardens. Although she was right on time, the other two judges were already there. One was Marian Sandefur who owned a small art gallery downtown, and the other was Gordon Littleton, a sculptor who had a national reputation. Ginny felt very outclassed in their presence.

She was surprised that both Marian and Gordon seemed to know about her.

"I think what you're doing with the children is wonderful," Marian said. "Too often adults tend to squelch kids' creativity. But you're encouraging them to give free rein to their imaginations."

"I second that," Gordon added. He was a husky young man, looking more like a pro-football player than an artist, with broad shoulders and well developed arms. Ginny supposed that came from chiseling away at stone all the time. Marian, on the other hand, was more ethereal looking, she thought, closer to how artists typically look. It turned out, however, she was more administrator than artist. She did not paint, but sought out young talent and encouraged it.

They discussed the rules of the contest and how the judging was to be done. They'd work independently, judging each entry on a numerical system. The contestants were given two hours to complete their entries, and the judges were on hand to make sure everyone was abiding by the contest rules.

By ten o'clock all the contestants had arrived and were given an area marked off on the beach where they could work individually or in groups. There were four categories, and the contestants were grouped according to whether they had chosen Politics, By the Sea, Leisure Time Activities, or Miscellaneous as their theme. Children under eight and children eight to fifteen were in separate groups. Ginny saw several of her regulars were participating. She'd have to be extra careful in her judging not to show any partiality.

At the sound of the bell, everyone hurriedly began, bringing buckets of water to their site to dampen the sand to the proper consistency. There were the conspicuous artists, working with the assurance and skill that comes from extensive training. Most, though, were amateurs who entered the contest more for the fun of it or in the hope that the cleverness of their idea would more than compensate for lack of artistic ability. Marian and Gordon had told Ginny that these non-artists often won because of the sheer merit of their idea or the humor and whimsy that caught the judge's eye. The sculptures were judged on the uniqueness of idea as much as artistic merit.

As Ginny walked between the marked-off areas, she was amazed at the level of expectation for both competitors and spectators. There was a holiday air about the event that was contagious. She was enjoying herself even more than she'd anticipated.

As she made her way through the area of feverish activity, she was surprised to see Naomi Catalano, dressed in cut-off jeans and faded tee shirt, working on a sculpture with two other women and a man. It was unexpected in a way, and yet Ginny pictured Naomi as someone who would participate in any offbeat experience, who relished nonconformity.

Naomi was so engrossed in their project, she didn't see Ginny, and Ginny didn't want to interrupt her. Besides she didn't want to flaunt any connections with participants for fear of the appearance of showing favoritism.

The two hours passed quickly, and although many finished their entries early, others were scrambling to make last minute adjustments as the final seconds ticked away. There were thirty-two sculptures in all so the judges were challenged to make their decisions by one o'clock.

Ginny was delighted by the cleverness and skill shown in the final products. The entries under Politics resembled political cartoons with caricatures of the president and other national leaders, most of them shown in a less than favorable light. One, in bas relief, showed the president dressed as a pirate pushing "Mr. Taxpayer" off the gangplank. Another was a miniature Capitol building with money flowing out from it in all directions with pigs on the receiving end to signify "pork."

The category By the Sea was popular with mermaids and King Neptune, ships and whales, and the image of a curvaceous lass getting a suntan in her string bikini. That one drew a lot of attention from the onlookers, especially the men. An enormous sand castle, at least five feet tall, with turrets and decorative parapets caught Ginny's attention. It was surrounded by a water-filled moat and a highly decorative gate marked the entrance. She thought she could simplify some of its unique ideas to use when she worked with the children.

Under Leisure Time Activities, various hobbies and sports were depicted, usually in a humorous way. Since many teams practiced in Florida, including the Cincinnati Reds in Sarasota, baseball was a popular theme. And beach volleyball was celebrated as well with portraits of Misty May-Treanor and Kerri Walsh along with an Olympic gold medal. Naomi's group had been in this category, and they had sculpted a bas relief head of Shakespeare with the caption "Join the Poetry-for-Lunch-Bunch." Ginny was intrigued by that.

The children's categories were a potpourri of ideas. Ginny recognized some of the children who worked with her, but she was determined not to let that sway her judgment. The truth was all the children's work was so uninhibited and fun, from Disney cartoons to favorite story book characters to a child's pet cat, it was hardest of all to judge. But she carefully gave each entry the fairest score she could determine. Finally the scores from all three judges were tallied, and the president of the Chamber of Commerce announced the winners to the crowd. Cheers went up as each name was read and checks given out. Naomi's group won second place in their category, and Naomi accepted the check for the group.

A couple of Ginny's "regulars," Anna with her mother, and Jason with his dad, came over to speak to her. None of her children had won cash awards. They were a little too young to be competitive yet, although she thought one day they would definitely be in contention. But these two had won honorable mentions.

"Look," said Anna, holding up her green ribbon for inspection.

"That's beautiful," Ginny said. "I'm so proud of you."

Anna's mother said, "Thanks to you, Ginny. You've been so great with the kids."

Jason's father agreed. "Jason can't wait to get down on the beach every afternoon," he said.

Jason had stuck his ribbon in his shorts pocket and was busy inspecting the large castle. Ginny had no doubt he'd be wanting to copy some of its elements the next time they met.

As the crowds began to disperse, Ginny sought out Naomi, who was talking to the others in her group.

She touched her arm. "Hi, Naomi, remember me?"

"Of course I do, Ginny! How are you? Didn't I see you judging this contest?"

"Yes, that was kind of a fluke. But it was such fun."

"Let me introduce my friends. This is Lucy Turner, Rebecca Stein, and Nicholas Frazier." Lucy was young and plump, Rebecca was probably in her forties and had a long, thin patrician face, and Nicholas was hard to judge. Ginny thought he might be in his sixties, but his skin was smooth and his features boyish in spite of his pure white hair that was long enough to blow about in an unruly fashion in the ocean breeze. His neatly trimmed beard and mustache, somewhat darker than his hair, seemed almost dichotomous as though he couldn't decide whether to be a nonconformist or not. They all smiled and said hello.

"I'm curious about your entry," Ginny said. "What's this 'lunch bunch' anyway?"

"Great," Naomi beamed. "That's exactly what we wanted, to stir up interest in it. A couple of others have asked, too. It's a loosely-knit bunch who like to write poetry. We get together downtown every Thursday noon at a little restaurant on First Street. That's so the ones who work can join us on their lunch hour. Some come every week; some only come once a month. We read our poems to each other and critique them. It's a wonderful support group and it's a great bunch of people, too."

"Sounds intriguing. And, by the way, congratulations on winning second place."

"That's another reason we entered the contest. We thought that if we could win some money, we'd start a fund to self publish a book with all our work in it. Why don't you join us, Ginny?"

"Yes, please do come," added Lucy. "We'd love to have you."

"But I haven't written any poetry."

"Come anyway," said Naomi. "You told me you used to write some. Maybe we could inspire you to start again. Or come just for the fellowship. We don't have any membership rules."

Ginny thought she might feel a little out of it with this group, but she was looking for ways to fill her time. Why not try it? She had nothing to lose.

"Sure, I'll come on Thursday. Be forewarned, though, I'll probably just be a bump on the log."

"You can be anything you want with us. We aren't looking to be impressed with erudite criticisms. All we want is the truth— your gut feelings about our poems. And if you don't have any feelings about them, that says a lot, too. We'll see you at Ramon's then."

"I'll be there, gut feelings and all," laughed Ginny.

They bid each other goodbye. As Ginny headed back to Tranquility Gardens, she walked along the edge of the surf, humming a little tune to herself. She hadn't felt this happy in a long time. This experience had validated her worth in the world she felt, even if it was something as simple as judging sand sculptures.

Just before she reached her building, she spotted something half buried in the wet sand that marked the edge of high tide. Brushing away loose sand, she uncovered the most beautiful olive shell she had yet seen. She thought of it as her reward for the day, one she would treasure. It would have its pride of place on her grandmother's cherry dresser where she could admire it whenever she felt down.

SEVENTEEN

It was Wednesday night before Ginny told Leland she'd be going out to lunch on Thursday.

"You'll have to get your own lunch tomorrow," she said during supper. She'd always been there to fix it for him, mainly because she had little reason not to.

"Oh?"

"Yes, I'm meeting Naomi Catalano downtown. Remember, she's that friend of Constance's who lives on Casey Key." She suddenly decided not to mention the purpose of the lunch. As far as he was concerned they were meeting to chat and perhaps shop together.

"Well, I'm glad to see you're finally making friends. You need to get out of your shell."

"I'm out on the beach every afternoon," she reminded him.

"I'm talking about adults. What kind of relationship can you have with eight-year-old kids?"

"A very special one." Ginny said emphatically. "But you're right. I need to get to know some people my own age, too. I'm working on it."

"Good."

The next morning she drove downtown, leaving early enough that the tourist season traffic jams wouldn't make her late. She was surprised to find a parking place in a city lot not far from Ramon's. She approached the restaurant wondering what she'd do if she didn't see a familiar face. She was apprehensive about this meeting. She'd never been with "arty" people before, and she wasn't at all sure she would feel comfortable with them. She liked Naomi very much, even though she was very different from anyone she'd ever known, but she still wondered if she wouldn't feel very out of place with this group.

She stopped for a moment outside the door, ostensibly to read the menu, but in reality to gather up the courage to walk in. Finally she entered and immediately saw Naomi sitting with several others at a large round table at the rear of the dining room.

"Hi," she greeted them as she reached the table. "Here I am." Wow, she thought, you'll really impress them with your wit and charm.

"Oh, good. I was so hoping you'd come. You remember Lucy and Nicholas." Naomi was beaming, and Ginny realized she was sincerely glad to see her. She nodded hello to the two she'd already met.

"And I'd like you to meet Corey Jamison and John Hildebrand. This is Ginny McAllister. Ginny wrote poetry years ago, and I'm trying to convince her to try her hand at it again. She's sure to be inspired when she hears ours. Right, guys?"

"Indubitably," grinned John. "Either that or she'll be convinced that modern poetry has really gone to the dogs."

"I'll try and keep an open mind," Ginny answered, sitting down. "But I think you'll find I'm pretty ignorant as to what constitutes good poetry." She took a seat between Lucy and Corey.

"It's all in the ear of the beholder," Nicholas said, unwrapping the napkin from his silverware and putting it on his lap. "What is music to one might be pure drivel to someone else. I think it's a lot like modern painting. One might be enthralled by an abstract that may look like garbage to the next person. I

115

think the important thing is sincerity. You can always tell when it's fake."

"We could go on all day about the merit or lack of it in modern poetry," Naomi said, "but what do you say we order lunch first or we'll never get out of here."

They all nodded and scrutinized the menu like youngsters who'd been gently scolded by their teacher. Ginny didn't know if Naomi had been chosen as their leader or whether she just naturally took charge in a group.

They chatted about a variety of things while they waited for their orders. It seemed to be a very congenial group with a lot of playful banter back and forth. Ginny picked up considerable information about them from their conversations. Corey worked at a photo shop on Main Street, and John was a public defender. Lucy was attending New College, a branch of the University of South Florida that encouraged students to design their own curriculum which included a lot of independent study. She was a literature major and very serious about her poetry. Nicholas was retired, evidently from some government job.

Once they began to eat, the group became serious. Corey pulled a sheaf of papers from her oversized shoulder bag, unfolded them and began to read her poetry. The others listened very intently, Naomi and Lucy making notes on small pads beside their plates. When she was done, the others discussed the poems, pointing out inappropriate or awkward words or phrases, suggesting alternatives that might present a sharper image or be smoother metrically.

And though they nearly demolished one poem, suggesting changes in every line and taking poor Corey back nearly to square one, it was done in such a constructive, loving way, that Corey seemed excited about the possibilities that were pointed out to her. She was anxious to get at her revision. Ginny could see that a fine line existed between inspiring and impeding in critiquing someone's writing. She knew how much of one's ego was bound up in a poem, and how fragile it was, even though she'd written very few. A flippant or off-hand remark could devastate the poet who had invested so much of herself in each line.

The reason she'd quit writing poetry so long ago was due mainly to thoughtless remarks that her father had made.

"Math will get you a lot farther in this world than some incomprehensible doggerel. Nobody's going to hire you because you write poetry. Be practical, girl." Practicality had always been his motto, and it seemed that Leland had carried it on. She'd always heard that men marry the image of their mothers, but it seemed to work the other way, too: like father, like husband.

It was now Nicholas' turn to read. Ginny was curious as to what kind of poem he would write. She thought he looked like a retired sea captain. No, that wasn't it. His face was too smooth to have been weathered by sun and sea over the years. Yet she couldn't imagine him behind a desk either. His flyaway hair was not trimmed in a businessman's cut. His flamboyant Hawaiian shirt inferred anything but a button-down image. And yet he had a certain self-effacing air that was anything but theatrical. He gave out mixed signals that defied categorizing.

Nicholas read like an embarrassed schoolboy who dreaded being judged by his peers. He seemed so self assured otherwise that she found it quite touching. His poems were simple, short, and filled with wonder at the beauty of nature. Ginny didn't think they were very good poems; they were a bit awkward, the meter didn't flow as it should, his choice of words could have been more imaginative. But what they did reveal was his remarkable sensitivity to the world around him. If his poems revealed the true man, Nicholas was one of those rare human beings in harmony with the natural world, who embraced all of nature's vagaries as wondrous, rather than threatening.

And, to Ginny, that seemed especially unusual in this of all places. Although people swarmed to the state to enjoy the outdoors, it seemed that they were engaged in a constant and formidable war against nature. The battle lines were drawn along the coastline where homeowners were locked in a losing struggle against erosion.

And there was always the threat of hurricanes. The season would soon begin, and Ginny knew that there was much concern, especially among those on the islands, that the Sarasota area was long overdue for a hurricane.

Along with sink holes, fire ants, and predatory alligators, it seemed that Florida had more than its share of natural hazards.

Yet Nicholas, in his poetry, reveled in nature's unpredictability. It was his theory that most of the problems that man encountered with nature were brought on by his own imprudence.

The poem mentioned the various forces of nature and summed up Nicholas's point of view in the last few lines:

> *"Why do we think*
> *foolish humans that we are,*
> *that we can overlook*
> *the natural laws that bind us*
> *to this earth.*
> *We will not only destroy*
> *the beauty we are blessed with,*
> *but ourselves as well."*

Ginny sat quietly as the others critiqued his poems and watched him closely as he listened to their suggestions. He graciously accepted any criticism about meter, length of line, anything to do with poetic form. But he adamantly refused to change the substance of their meaning, even when Lucy pointed out he might have gone a little overboard in claiming that hurricanes were beautiful.

"Have you ever been in one?" he asked her.

"God, no. And I hope I never am."

"Well, I have, and let me tell you that there is beauty in their awesomeness. It's man's stupidity in building on the beaches that makes them so threatening. As long as we go against nature, we make all sorts of problems for ourselves."

"What do you want to do," Lucy's voice had a slight edge, "go back to living like the cave men?"

"Not hardly. But most of the so-called primitive people had a lot more respect for nature than we do. And they knew how to live in harmony with it, not constantly do battle with it."

"Well, I think our quality of life is a hell of a lot better now."

"I'm not at all sure of that." Nicholas spoke softly but with complete assurance. "Florida is rapidly going down the tube, and we all sit around and shrug our shoulders over it."

"You're overreacting, Nicholas." Corey spoke for the first time.

"I wish a few more would overreact before it's too late."

"Order in the court," Naomi knocked on the table twice with her iced tea glass. "Let's not get into politics, guys. We'll save that discussion for the 'Save Our Bays Association.' Does anyone else have any suggestion for Nicholas that is strictly poetic?"

The group was silent.

"Okay, then, it's getting late. What say we adjourn until next week."

Everyone began putting together all their papers in preparation to leave. Naomi came over to Ginny.

"I'm delighted you came. I hope you'll come regularly."

"I'd like to. I didn't contribute anything, but maybe after a while I'll feel more comfortable about speaking up."

"Sure you will. Are you going to try your hand at writing

something?"

"I might. I'll see if I'm bowled over by inspiration this week," Ginny replied.

"You can't wait around for it to walk up and bite you on the you-know-what. Sometimes you have to sit down and sweat it out."

"Well . . . we'll see."

"I've gotta run. I'm parked at a meter that I'm sure has run out. See you next week, Ginny." And Naomi hurried out of the restaurant.

Nicholas walked over after Naomi left. "Welcome to our little group. We may sound like we're angry with each other, but we're really not. It's all part of the entertainment."

"I found it . . . lively I guess is the word," Ginny said.

"It gets even livelier sometimes. Please bring some of your work and join in."

"I don't have anything now, but maybe I'll give it a try." Even though she said that, she wasn't at all sure she would.

"That's the secret of it. We all keep trying even if we're not completely successful. It's the challenge that counts. Naomi is the only real pro in the group. The rest of us just do it as a pastime, so don't worry that we'll be too hard on you." Nicholas grinned and patted her on the shoulder to reassure her.

"I admit it does worry me some."

"Well, I talk a good ball game, but I suppose you noticed that I'm a little nervous when I read. But, really, there's no sense in getting all intense about it. At least I keep telling myself that." He laughed heartily, running his fingers through his hair, combing it back from his forehead. It was the gesture of a man unused to contending with long hair. Ginny guessed that he'd only recently retired and the hair and wild shirt were his way of celebrating his liberation from the desk brigade.

Leland had developed his own idiosyncrasies. He flat out

refused to wear a tie now or black socks. He even wore white socks to church services.

"Have you been in Florida long?" she asked.

"No. I was with a state bureaucracy for years up north, and I just moved to Sarasota a couple of years ago when I retired. You can probably tell I was not a quiet, obedient public servant. I'm afraid I ran off at the mouth some, and that accounts for my early retirement."

"I found your ideas quite provocative. I haven't been here long, but there's always a lot in the paper about the concerns on the keys. As a matter of fact I live in a high rise on Crescent Beach."

"Have you ever seen pictures of the way Siesta Key used to be fifty years ago?"

"No."

"It would make you cry."

"Quite frankly, this isn't my choice of a way to live. I'd rather be where there's a mix of age groups."

"You mean you had no input?" Nicholas gave her a look that said how could she allow such a thing?

She realized she'd made it sound as if Leland had run roughshod over her. He'd acted in what he thought was her best interest. "Not at all. I was laid up with a smashed-up knee in Ohio, and he thought the sooner he could get me down here, the better off I'd be."

"I see." But he still looked skeptical.

"Well, I must go." Although she didn't really have a reason to hurry, she felt she better not continue the conversation. "Will you be here next week?" Now why did she ask that?

"Oh, sure. I get a kick out of this group, and I try to make it every time. I'll see you then?"

"I think so. Goodbye now." She picked up her purse and walked hurriedly out of the restaurant.

EIGHTEEN

At dinner that night Leland was full of himself. "I feel like I hit the jackpot today." He uncharacteristically dished himself an extra helping of mashed potatoes. "First I broke eighty on the golf course, and then I met a man on the third floor who invited me to go out on his boat. Pat Patterson's his name, and he has one of those pricey jobs with all the fancy fishing equipment." Leland coveted such a boat, but they cost a small fortune and the upkeep was enormous.

"That's wonderful. Is this a one-time-only invite or are you going to be a regular guest?"

"This is for next Monday. I don't know whether he'll ask me again or not. But at least I should have better luck out in the Gulf. Fishing near shore has been pretty disappointing lately."

"Why is that?"

"Too many people, I guess."

"That goes for traffic, too. I got held up at the north bridge this morning."

"It happens all the time. How was your lunch with your friend?"

"Very nice. She's quite interesting. I think we'll meet every week for lunch, in fact. It gets both Naomi and me out of the house, and I guess we're both the kind who need a little prodding." She couldn't look him in the eye as she said it but concentrated on cutting up her steak instead. Someday she would admit to him what she was really doing on Thursdays, but she wasn't ready yet. She hated deception, but she hated even more being made to feel foolish.

In the mornings, when Leland was golfing, Ginny tried her hand at writing poetry. She went to the library where she found some Emily Dickinson collections and some anthologies of recent work by women. It had been many years since she'd read much poetry, and she was excited to find she'd had an erroneous concept of it as a whole. She'd been sure that it was all very vague, written in such obscure language that no one but the poet could possibly understand its meaning.

But instead she found that much of it was entirely the opposite. And the richness of the language, the emotions a few well chosen words could evoke caught her imagination. But it looked so deceptively simple. She found it was a very frustrating experience to write a poem. She knew what she wanted to say, she could feel the emotion she wanted to express mounting inside her, but how to put it down on paper?

She found herself lingering for long periods of time over the choice of a single word. Because that one word had to be just right. She would write a few lines at a time only to discard them later.

Writing poetry wasn't a lark, she decided, but damn hard work. She would feel exhausted after a couple of hours' effort, as though she'd been engaged in physical labor. She was tempted to forget the whole idea, but she'd accepted a challenge and was determined to meet it. Besides, she'd enjoyed being with the group so much, she didn't want to give it up. And she couldn't keep going indefinitely without contributing some of her own works.

She was going to write a poem if it killed her! She just didn't want it to be so awful she would be mortified to read it.

She still met the children in the afternoons on the beach. Now, instead of having them simply build sand castles, she was encouraging them to work on other kinds of sculptures, too. Sometimes they would make "sea creatures" like turtles or fish. Sometimes they would recreate cartoon figures that they saw in the funny papers each day. There was a regular core group of children who came nearly every day, while others wandered in and out. The regulars now took over much of the organizing which gave her time to sit back and think about her poetry. She knew she wanted to write something about the sea; it seemed to her it could serve as the perfect metaphor for life's disillusionments.

On Monday morning, Leland was up before dawn. Pat Patterson was leaving at six for the all-day fishing trip, and two others from Tranquility Gardens were joining them. When he left, Ginny could not go back to sleep. After reading the paper, she tried to work some more on her poetry. It seemed to be going nowhere.

At nine-thirty, feeling totally thwarted, she called Naomi.

"Hi, Naomi, this is Ginny McAllister. Say, I've been working on a poem, and I feel like I'm beating my head against the wall. Any chance you could help me if I came down there?"

"Sure. And why don't you plan to stay for lunch? Nicholas is coming over then so we can talk about the book we want to put together with our prize money. Maybe you could give us some ideas."

"Oh, I don't want to intrude on your meeting."

Naomi laughed her contagious laugh. "Heavens, hon, you're not intruding. After all, we partially have you to thank for awarding us the prize. And maybe you can contribute some great marketing ideas. We need all the input we can get."

Ginny spent extra time making up her face and getting dressed. She didn't like the first skirt and blouse she put on, so she took them off and chose a more becoming outfit, aware all the while that her behavior was out of character.

Since coming to Florida, she'd taken less interest in how she looked, reasoning that the wind undid any hairdo she arranged and that the heat and dampness soon gave her a wilted appearance anyway. She tried to assure herself that she was anxious to earn Naomi's approval, but she knew that was patently ridiculous. Naomi was the last one to be impressed by how a person looked. Who was she kidding?

As she drove down Route 41 toward Casey Key, she felt wonderful. It was one of those perfect days that the Florida Chamber of Commerce touts in their ads: pleasantly warm but without the normal mugginess; vivid blue skies with only a wandering puff of cloud here and there to break the monotony; a light breeze that caresses but doesn't whip open wrap-around skirts or destroy carefully coiffed hair.

She'd managed to get across Stickney Point Bridge without having to wait while it was raised for a boat. That was a good omen. And the traffic on 41 seemed lighter than usual. It probably meant that everyone was out on the beaches enjoying this extraordinary day. She felt free, released from her normal schedule. Leland had said they wouldn't be home until late, not to cook dinner for him.

As she drove down Casey Key, she felt a twinge of envy. She loved this island with its intriguing mix of houses and jungle. No high rise intruded upon the view or broke through the canopy of trees.

She pulled into Naomi's drive and knocked on the door.

Naomi answered dressed in short shorts and a halter. Even though she was no longer young, she had a figure that let her get away with such outfits. Ginny felt a little foolish in her conservative skirt and blouse.

Naomi gave her a hug. "So you're really working on some poetry. Come on in and let's take a look at it."

They settled in on the porch. Ginny loved this place. She felt more relaxed in its cool shadows than any place she could think of. The fronds of palm trees rubbed against the roof in the breeze, making a soft whooshing sound that could have lulled her to sleep. The overgrown lot was alive with the muted noises of the tropics: chirping birds, the rustling of leaves by unseen creatures, the incessant chirr of the peepers singing in unison. A small lizard climbed the screen next to her in its unceasing search for insects.

Naomi went to the kitchen and brought back a tray with coffee pot, cups and a plate with wedges of avocado, pineapple, cantaloupe and honeydew.

"This is pretty rough," Ginny said as she pulled out a folded paper from her purse. "I know what I want to say, but I don't know how to say it."

Naomi read it over, and Ginny tried to read her face for clues to her reaction. But Naomi's features were as noncommittal as a poker player's. She laid it on her lap and smoothed the wrinkles out with her hand. "You've got some unique ideas here. Let's see if we can state them in a more poetic manner."

So she didn't like it much. Ginny was disappointed, though she knew her attempt was a long way from being polished. She was going to have to learn to accept criticism without getting uptight about it. They spent the rest of the morning taking the poem word by word and analyzing it. They were giving it the final touches when the doorbell rang.

Naomi excused herself and came back a moment later followed by Nicholas. Ginny couldn't believe it was noon already. She checked her watch and saw that it was actually ten past.

"Well, hello Ginny." Nicholas seemed pleasantly surprised to see her. He seated himself next to her in a tangerine director's chair. "Are you a member of our book planning group?" He was wearing camping shorts and a striped shirt that was a bit more subdued than the ones he'd worn before.

"She came over for help with a poem, and I asked her to stay on for our meeting," Naomi said standing in the doorway. "I thought she might give us some ideas about distributing our book. Excuse me a minute while I get lunch. I fixed some seafood salad early this morning so it won't take long."

Nicholas leaned toward her. She could smell his cologne, an unusual ambrosial scent she couldn't identify. Leland always wore spicy scented cologne that was more pungent than this. "Are you going to let me take a look at what you've been working on?"

She hesitated. "I'm not sure it's ready for public consumption," she laughed hoping he wouldn't press her.

"No poem ever is," he said. "But sometimes you just have to let go anyway."

"Well, okay, if you promise not to laugh." She tried to say it jokingly, but she was quite serious.

"I wouldn't dream of laughing unless the poet intended it," he said in all seriousness.

She reached in her purse and pulled out the carelessly folded page that contained the rewritten poem. She'd stuck it there hurriedly when Naomi went to answer the doorbell. She started to hand it to him and then stopped.

"We've written over it so much I don't think you could make head or tails of it. I'll read it to you," she said.

Her voice trembled with nervousness as she read. "It's called 'The Order of Things.' " She cleared her throat and read on.

"The murky form of seaweed hangs
suspended in its liquid world
undulating gently with each swell,
yet scarcely moving.
The churlish waves and fretful wind
pass harmlessly above its mass
unable to impose their will.

127

How does this flotsam manage
to maintain such equanimity
in turmoil's face, while I,
struggling on the water's top,
am pounded unremittingly
by each and every wave,
then flung contemptuously
upon the shore?"

Nicholas didn't say anything immediately, and Ginny had a sinking feeling that he thought it was so bad, he couldn't think of anything tactful to say.

He kneaded his hands together thoughtfully for a minute, and then looked at her questioningly, his expression one of real concern.

"That's very profound. Do you honestly feel that way?"

"Well . . . of course. I sometimes think we humans get the short end of the stick. Or maybe it's more that we have the brains and ability to recognize the fact that most things are beyond our control." Ginny hadn't meant to say all this, but after all, he'd asked her. She was beginning to understand how reading poetry could lead to discussions that wouldn't normally come up in every day conversations.

"You feel that life has just pushed you around, and you have no control over it?" Nicholas moved slightly closer to look directly into her eyes.

She was beginning to feel uncomfortable. This conversation was getting too personal. She knew that any poetry worthy of the name was infused with the poet's feelings. It was a cathartic process, at least for her. And yet she felt that it was something distinct from her, that she could hold it at arm's length as a work of art and not allow it to represent her as a person. Or could she? Wasn't it in fact her secret heart that she elected to wear on her sleeve? She realized she couldn't distance herself from her poems and maintain their integrity. This was a sudden revelation, and it alarmed her.

"I guess it's my subconscious speaking out," she said, hedging. "It's just sort of a vague feeling I have about life . . ." Her voice trailed off for she knew that was untrue. Instead of looking Nicholas in the eye, she was staring at the paper, rolling the edges of it nervously between her fingers, wondering how to change the subject.

He seemed to sense her discomfort. He sat back in his chair, rubbed his hands together and said, "Well, I wonder what fabulous dessert Naomi will serve today. She's famous for her desserts, you know."

Just then Naomi appeared in the doorway. "Come on, the food's on. Let's get with it and talk about our book."

Whatever Naomi did seemed to have a special touch. The small glass-topped round table under a large window was set with hand-woven place mats in tangerine, a color accent she used throughout the house. The dishes didn't match, they were odds and ends of hand-painted antique plates, but they all shared the same palette of soft greens. A large irregular shaped hand-hewn wooden bowl held the seafood salad, and graceful goblets were filled with white wine. In a small glass dish in the center, three lemon-colored hibiscuses floated in water. A basket of hot rolls was on the window sill.

"This table almost isn't big enough for three," she apologized, "but it's a job to unload everything from the drop-leaf table, so I figured we could manage." The drop-leaf was piled high with stacks of magazines and behind them was a large collection of exotic paperweights.

When they were seated, they were so close together that Nicholas' leg touched Ginny's, the thin fabric of her skirt barely keeping skin from rubbing skin, and it was impossible for her to move away as her chair backed up to the wall.

Throughout the meal they talked about the book of poems they wanted to put together. Rather, Naomi and Nicholas talked because Ginny knew very little about it. She was keenly aware of the pressure of Nicholas' knee against hers; every time he shifted position it would nudge her slightly, but she was sure it was in all innocence because of their cramped positions. She should have put it out of her mind, but she couldn't. She tried to appear as if she were completely engrossed in their conversation, but, in reality, she only half heard them. Her whole body became tense in anticipation of the next light nudge. She felt like a ninth grader who was fixated on the boy sitting beside her, but she couldn't seem to help herself.

"What do you think, Ginny?" Naomi's voice broke through her preoccupation.

"Oh, I'm sorry, I'm afraid my mind was wandering. What was the question?" She could feel herself blush and hoped the others wouldn't notice.

"Should we include some work from everybody in the book, or should we hold a contest to choose only the best poems?"

"What if someone's poems are so bad it would embarrass the group? I mean speaking for myself, I'm not at all sure I could be objective enough to know if my stuff is garbage or not. And I wouldn't want to think mine would be included even if they're terrible."

"You don't have to worry about that, Ginny," Nicholas said. "I've only just seen the one, of course, but it definitely is not garbage." Just then he shifted in his chair, and his knee pushed hard against her thigh for a second. There was no indication in his expression that he even noticed it. But Ginny could still feel the contact after his leg had pulled back. Her body had become acutely conscious of touch, and she was suddenly aware of the metallic hardness of the fork in her hand, the smoothness of the linen napkin as she wiped her mouth, the cold, wet solidity of the goblet as she sipped the wine.

"I don't think anyone in the group has anything to be embarrassed about," Naomi said. "Some are more polished writers, of course, but I think everyone has something that would add to the collection. I think all members should submit a bunch of poems and a judge should select the best five from each person."

"That sounds like a fair way to handle it then." Ginny wanted the discussion to be over. She wanted to get away from the table.

"I'll go get the dessert," Naomi said rising. "We can talk about how we're going to market the book over that. I made some key lime pie just for you all. Did I tell you I have a key lime tree in the yard?"

"What did I tell you?" Nicholas smiled at Ginny.

"Excuse me, too," Ginny said struggling awkwardly to her feet. "I'll be right back." She hurried toward the kitchen where Naomi was dishing up the pie.

"Where do I find the bathroom?" she asked.

"Down the hall, first door on the left."

She hurried to it, closed the door and sank onto the edge of the tub. She laid her head on her arm on the side of the sink and was aware that her heart was pounding rapidly. Was she coming down with something? Her face felt flushed. She sat quietly for several minutes trying to regain her composure.

She stood up, dampened a washcloth with cold water and wiped her face with it. She stared in the mirror, trying to imagine how others saw her. Her blue-green eyes were ordinary; they would never command a second glance. Her mouth was her best feature, she thought, since she knew that her smile tended to light up her whole face, or at least she'd been told that by friends. She tried to remember to smile as much as possible around people because she knew she appeared almost morose otherwise.

She was always shocked to see snapshots of herself that had caught her off guard, unsmiling and looking rather grim, even when she knew she hadn't felt that way. Her hair had begun to turn gray early, and she'd stopped tinting it, first because it was too much trouble after her leg was hurt, and then because she decided she liked it. All in all, she felt she had aged rather well.

She had to get back to Naomi and Nicholas or they would think she was ill. She tried to push all turmoil from her mind, afraid she was going to make a fool of herself if she wasn't careful. When she walked back into the living room, she was greatly relieved to see them sitting on the porch eating their pie and talking earnestly.

"Come on out here," Naomi said. "We're discussing how to market our book and we're short of ideas. Have you ever done any selling?"

Ginny made a point to sit so that Naomi was between her and Nicholas. She picked up her pie from a tray table, and tried a bite. It was delicious, the unique tangy taste of lime topped with whipped cream. Even the crust was perfect. The best key lime pie she'd eaten.

"I did sell Girl Scout cookies years ago. Does that count?" She smiled at Naomi, avoiding Nicholas' eyes.

But he answered anyway. "Sure. Cookies, poetry, socks, cars; I guess selling is selling." Nicholas brought out a pipe and a packet of tobacco from the pocket of his poplin jacket. "Would you girls mind if I smoke?"

They both shook their heads no. He made a little ceremony of cleaning out the old tobacco into an ashtray, tamping in the new, and lighting up. "This was the only way I could give up cigarettes," he said. "I had to have something to do with my hands, and I don't inhale this." It was so unusual to see someone smoking a pipe any more. But somehow it fit Nicholas, making him look like an old-time mariner. And Ginny had always liked the smell of a pipe.

"I think I'll join you." Naomi went into the house and came back with two of her hand-rolled cigarettes. She held one up wordlessly to Ginny who declined. After she lit up, the sweet scent of pipe tobacco and marijuana hovered over the group, enveloping them in a cloying cloud that made Ginny's head light. Could breathing in the smoke make her feel this way? She did feel a little strange. God, what would Leland think?

They discussed their marketing plan, the conversation becoming more laconic as the afternoon progressed. Finally Naomi said, "Remember, we can't do too much till we have the book in hand. Ginny, I know you are brand new to the group, and we shouldn't jump on you right away with a bunch of things to do, but could you talk to some printers and get some estimates for us? Most of the others work and haven't much time for things like that."

"Sure," she replied, flattered that they wanted to make her an integral part of the group.

"And Nicholas, how about finding us a judge. That's the very first thing we have to do."

"Will do."

Naomi eased back in her chair, languidly crossing one outstretched leg over the other, completely relaxed now. "I guess that does it for now. I think we've done a lot today, don't you?"

Ginny assumed this was Naomi's polite way of signaling they should leave now. She'd been there over five hours.

"Let me help you with the dishes," she said automatically, the gracious guest.

"Oh, no, of course not," Naomi's voice was slow and sleepy.

Ginny knew it was time to go. "I'll see you at noon on Thursday then. I really appreciate all your help, and the lunch was delicious."

Naomi rose slowly to her feet, taking a deep puff on the stub end of the joint. "You're going to be a good poet, Ginny, if you keep working at it. You'll be a real asset to our group."

Ginny nodded shyly, not knowing how to respond to this compliment. Maybe Naomi was only saying this because she was high, but she hoped not. She hoped it was really true.

Nicholas stood up then and put out his hand to help Ginny up. "I second that motion," he said. She hadn't had so much flattery in years.

"I was wondering," he continued, "if I could possibly hitch a ride with you back to Sarasota. My car is in the garage so I took a taxi this morning. I was going to call one to come get me, but it could take them forever to get here. Would it inconvenience you?"

"Oh, no, of course not," Ginny said, wishing she could think of a reasonable excuse to turn him down. But she couldn't without being rude.

Nicholas graciously opened the door of the Buick for her and she slid behind the wheel. She wasn't used to such gallantry; Leland hadn't opened a car door for her since their honeymoon as far as she could remember.

NINETEEN

As they drove back up the Key he said, "Doesn't this place get to you? I think Sarasota is barren looking. I always thought of Florida as jungly, and I was very disappointed to find it wasn't. But Casey Key is different. I don't know how these people managed to preserve all this wonderful growth, but it's a gem."

She glanced at him surprised. "You must have been reading my mind. I'd give my eyeteeth to live here, but I suppose even a shack would be worth a fortune."

"Let's just say it's not for those on a limited income. I know that Naomi bought hers for a song thirty-some years ago, and she could make a mind-boggling profit on it. But she doesn't want to leave."

"I don't blame her."

They rode in silence till they reached the small bridge that took them back to the mainland. "Oh," said Nicholas, "I forgot to tell you where I live. I hope it isn't too much out of your way."

"I'm in no rush," she answered, "my husband won't be home for dinner tonight."

"I live in a little house just off Clark Road, out toward Beneva," he said.

"That's hardly out of my way at all." Clark Road was the eastern extension of Stickney Point Road which was the southern bridge to the Key.

"Your husband's not retired then?" he asked.

"Oh, yes, the company forced him to retire early, but he's loving every minute of it. He's out on a fishing boat today."

"Children?"

"Just one, a son in Cleveland. No grand kids though."

"Oh, that's too bad. They're such a joy. Well, your time will come."

"I'm afraid not. They informed me recently they don't want children." My God, why was she running her mouth this way?

He shook his head in sympathy. "What a shame. You'll have to adopt some neighborhood kids to take their place."

"There aren't any neighborhood kids. We live in one of those all-adult condos. That's why I go out on the beach every afternoon and help the kids there make sand sculptures."

Nicholas sat forward and looked at her intently. "Oh, so you're the sand castle lady. I read the article about you, but I hadn't put two and two together. Guess I didn't look at the picture very closely. I was very impressed."

"Impressed? With what?"

He thought about it a minute, stroking his beard. "With your free spiritedness, I guess."

Ginny started to laugh. "That's the first time in my life that anyone called me a free spirit. I'm afraid I'm anything but."

"Perhaps you don't know yourself as well as you think you do."

She sat silently, feeling the color rise again in her face. They were stopped in a long line of traffic next to the Sarasota Square Mall waiting for the light to change. From this point north, the streets always became more and more clogged. The sign for the shopping center read "Antique Show featuring dealers from four states, March 19-20-21."

"Look," Nicholas pointed to the sign, "I hadn't realized there was an antique show on and this is the last day. I've been look-ing for a certain tool for my collection and haven't been able to find it. Would you by any chance be interested in spending a few minutes in the mall?"

What could she say? She'd already told him she was free for the rest of the afternoon. Surely he was just being congenial anyway. Whatever subtle undercurrents she thought were there had to be a figment of her overblown imagination.

She turned the corner onto Beneva Road and drove into the mall parking lot. "I always enjoy antique shows," she said, "although the few pieces I have were all handed down through the family. But it's fun to see what I could get for my things now, not that I'd ever sell them."

"Those are the best kind, the ones that you have a history for. Most of my tool collection was handed down from my grandfather who was a carpenter, but I do like to add a piece now and then. Woodworking is my hobby, so I have a special affinity for tools anyway."

Ginny was happy to find a parking spot in the crowded lot. In the mall the tables were set up end to end throughout the spoke-shaped walkways. Every kind of antique imaginable was displayed from old books to furniture. Ginny wished she could get rid of some of the modern things in their condo and replace the chrome and glass with the richness of walnut or oak. But she was thankful she still had a handful of her favorite pieces to warm up the cold whiteness of the rooms with the patina of fine old wood.

She wandered a few paces behind Nicholas who browsed lovingly at each table. Most men she knew, including Leland, disliked shopping and would do so only under protest. He would go to a store when he had a specific object to buy, would purchase that item and leave immediately.

Nicholas, on the other hand, picked up objects frequently, examining them closely, running his blunt, thick fingers over them as if reading Braille, and then put them back down almost reluctantly. Sometimes he would even sniff a small item, as if able to ascertain its past by its musty odor. It was fascinating to watch him. He leafed through yellowing books, peered into humpbacked sea chests, held hand-painted china plates up to the light. And when he came to a table covered with old tools, it was as if he were mesmerized by them. He had to examine each and every piece, testing moveable parts, fingering mars and scratches, comparing weights of similar tools.

Finally he selected an old wooden vise and purchased it. He looked up startled as if surprised to see Ginny standing there. "Have you had a chance to look around and see everything?" he asked.

"Oh, yes. This is quite a show. Some of these things are really tempting, but I just don't have the space any more."

"I really don't either. But I'm kind of a compulsive buyer when I find something I want. They'll find me someday buried under a mountain of stuff. Mostly old nonessential stuff, too. I don't buy electronic gadgets and things that most people want; just beautiful old things that have no real usefulness. But anyway, how about a cup of coffee? The smoke from Naomi's weed nearly put me to sleep."

Ginny hesitated for just a second and then said, "Sure."

They went to one of the sandwich bars for their coffee and sat at one of the little round metal tables that bordered the mall.

"You haven't said much about yourself except that you used to work for a state government."

"Up in Vermont. I was a civil servant, into environmental work. Actually, I wasn't too civil. That's what got me in trouble."

"That explains your poetry then."

"If it hadn't been my vocation, it would have been my avocation. I feel pretty strongly about the environment."

"So do I. I just feel helpless to do anything."

"Don't we all. But we have to start turning that around."

She had been aware from the start that Nicholas wore no ring, but she had to ask anyway. "Are you married?"

He stared into his cup, holding it tightly with both hands. "My wife died five years ago from cancer."

"I'm so sorry." Ginny said nothing for a couple of minutes. "But you have children? You mentioned grand kids."

He smiled. "I have a son and two daughters, but only one lives nearby, my youngest daughter Marcy. I have five grandchildren, two in town. God, that makes me feel old. No, on the contrary, when I'm around them, I feel quite young. The oldest is eight."

"How lucky you are." Ginny said, thinking what a wonderful grandfather Nicholas would make.

"I think so."

A comfortable silence fell over them. Ginny was aware that a line had been crossed, an invisible line that marks the boundary between acquaintances and friends, and it worried her a bit. She'd never felt this relaxed with any man other than Leland since her marriage. There'd always been a certain holding back, a slight reserve, even with men she'd known for years. That was just the way it was. Recently she'd read articles in magazines that claimed it was not only proper but rewarding to have close male friends in the same sense that women have close female friends. But she'd never been able to do that. Her generation of women had been conditioned to keep men who weren't their husband at arm's length.

But perhaps the magazines were right. Nicholas had qualities that greatly attracted her, a quiet sincerity, a sweet disposition, a sensitivity unusual in a man. If Nicholas had been a woman, she would have become fast friends without hesitation. And that was not to say he was effeminate in any way; he was not. But he was not macho either. But could she, she wondered, as the magazines suggested, have a strong friendship with him that was platonic? That was what she desperately wanted. But her experience at lunch warned her that it might not be possible.

Nicholas checked his watch. "I've kept you longer than I meant to. I'd better be getting home."

Because of the heavy traffic, it took them another twenty minutes to get to his house although it was only a short distance from the shopping center. He lived in a small white stucco house, a typical Florida tract house that Ginny considered ugly; a box without imagination. What made it stand out from its neighbors was the attempt to impose a natural look on the small lot. While the other houses on the street had little landscaping except the usual mangy grass—lawns did poorly in this climate without constant care—his was planted with Indian Rosewood trees with large spreading branches that hovered over the roof, an orchid tree full of lavender blooms, as well as bushes and flowers surrounded by a lawn of groundcover. It was like a minuscule oasis in a desert of indifference and neglect.

"It's lovely," Ginny said, as he thanked her for the ride.

"I can't afford to live on Casey Key, but I like to pretend I have a tiny corner of the jungle here. My backyard is even thicker than this. It's called escapism."

"I call it smart. If other people want to sit out in the hot sun, let them. I choose trees any time."

"Well, I'll see you Thursday then."

She had to think a minute what he meant. "Oh, you mean the group at Ramon's. Right."

It was after nine before Leland came home. "Look at this," he said, putting a bucket of fish on the kitchen counter. "I tell you the fishing is great out there. It seems they almost want to jump into the boat."

"Looks good." Ginny put her arms around his waist and

hugged him. "Hon, it's been a long day. Why don't you stick them in the fridge till morning and let's go to bed now." She gave him a kiss and another hug so he'd be sure not to miss her meaning.

"I'm wide awake and I want to get these babies cleaned now. The quicker I freeze them, the better they'll be." Could it be that he misunderstood what she was saying, or was he turning her down?

She dropped her arms at once and stepped back. She'd normally accept such rejection without comment or much disappointment. But this time she would not.

"Leland, I want to make love with you. I do not want to be turned down."

He looked baffled. "Okay, okay, I thought you were just offering for my benefit. Let me wrap them up and put them in the refrigerator, take a quick shower, and I'll be there in a minute."

She got undressed and slipped into bed without her nightgown. About ten minutes later Leland came in, put on his pajamas and got in beside her. She snuggled up beside him.

"What's this, no nightgown? What's come over you, Ginny?" he said as he stroked her breasts.

"Shut your mouth and concentrate on the business at hand," she whispered.

They made vigorous love, and Ginny was more aggressive than usual. Instead of rolling away from Leland when they were done, she lay close beside him.

"What's got into you?" Leland propped himself up on his elbow to look at her. "I haven't seen that much liveliness in you in a long time."

"I don't know," she answered, not convinced she was telling the truth. "I'm feeling better lately. My knee doesn't hurt much any more. Maybe the fact you were gone all day made me miss you. Whatever, why question it? Why not just enjoy it?"

"I did, believe me." He dropped back down on his back and within minutes was snoring.

But Ginny lay awake for a long time. She kept going over and over the day in her mind, but the more she thought about it, the more confused she became.

At last blessed sleep came, but Nicholas was in her dreams. She dreamt that the two of them were stranded on an island which was covered in thick jungle. She ran into the jungle to hide from him, and was consumed with disappointment when he did not follow her.

TWENTY

The next day Leland went back to golfing in the morning and fishing from a pier in the afternoon. He'd gotten up very early to clean and prepare the mackerel for freezing before he left. Their supply of frozen fish was nearly enough to feed an army. They were going to have to start giving it away soon.

Ginny went grocery shopping in the morning since they were low on everything but fish. She'd always gone to the Winn-Dixie on Clark Road, and today was no exception. But as she pushed her cart up and down the aisles, trying to concentrate on her shopping list, she was also conscious of the fact that she was watching the door to see if Nicholas would walk in. He lived only a few blocks away, and it seemed likely he would shop here.

Once she thought she saw him from the back leaning over the frozen food displays. Her whole body was alert, on edge. But when the man straightened up, she saw he didn't resemble Nicholas at all. She hastily finished her shopping and rushed to the checkout counter. The cashier was half through scanning her groceries when she remembered she had planned to have pork chops for supper. It was too late now. She'd fix hamburgers or something.

At lunch Leland talked about his golf game and about the trip the day before. Ginny sat silently gazing out at the parking lot.

"Hey," he said, "are you with me?"

"Huh?" She was shaken from her reverie.

"You haven't heard a word I've said."

"Yes, I have. Roger said the golf course wasn't being maintained properly, and Ben said you all should write a protest letter." So who cares? she thought. She'd always thought golf was a ridiculous game anyway.

"So they asked me to head up a committee to round up as many signatures as possible on our letter. We want to really stir them up so they'll do something."

"Good, honey," she said absently, "go for it."

After he'd gone out again, she read for a while and then changed to her bathing suit. She carefully covered her body with sun block, put on her large-brimmed hat, gathered up her bucket of tools, and walked out to the beach.

Several of the regulars were there already, the children who came daily to build castles with her. Tommy, an eight-year-old towhead with shockingly blue eyes that glowed like lapis lazuli in his darkly tanned face, ran up to her.

"Hey, where were you yesterday Mrs. McAllister? We waited for you, but you didn't show up."

"Sorry, I was busy and couldn't get away. But that doesn't mean you can't go on without me."

"Oh, sure, we know that. But it isn't as much fun when you aren't here."

Ginny couldn't remember when she'd been as warmed by a comment as she was by Tommy's simple statement. It put a whole new perspective on her day.

She grabbed Tommy's hand and walked toward the others who were waiting. "Let's go," she said. "We're going to build a humongous castle today." She loved using the children's exaggerated vocabulary.

She had a humongous need right now to dig into the sand

and make the biggest and best castle they were capable of building.

They all worked with a kind of frenetic energy, the children taking a cue from Ginny. There were six of them, five of them who were regulars, and one other child who was new to the group.

"And what is your name?" Ginny asked the newcomer as they worked side by side. The girl, who seemed quite shy, almost whispered, "Beth."

"Would you like to use this spatula and cup, Beth?"

"Thank you," she said diffidently. She appeared to be about seven years old, and Ginny was impressed with her dexterity and artistic skill. The child had real ability to manipulate the sand into interesting and imaginative shapes. After working with the children for so long, Ginny could recognize talent immediately. And Beth had talent.

They managed to produce their most elaborate castle ever that afternoon. It was a U-shaped building with magnificent crenellated towers at every corner, a large moat spanned by a drawbridge (which was supported by a piece of driftwood), an ornate portico at the entrance, and arched windows throughout.

Beth, in her quiet reserved way, urged the others on toward perfection.

"Look, Tommy, that wall is a little crooked there," she said. "Why don't you use the spatula to make it a little smoother." And she handed him Ginny's now well-worn kitchen tool that had been relegated to the beach.

He took it eagerly and began patting the wall into shape.

Beth showed Anna a new way to construct the crenellation with square piece of driftwood she found. Instead of painstakingly cutting out the shapes with the small plastic knife Ginny had in her tool bucket, Beth merely pressed the driftwood down into the sand parapets at regular intervals to create the notches.

Rather than resent her perfectionism, the children seemed inspired by her. Ginny hoped she would come regularly.

"You will come back, won't you?" Ginny asked her as the group broke up for the day.

"Oh, yes. I had fun today."

The next afternoon, true to her word, Beth returned. This time the group decided to sculpt a mermaid instead of a castle. They were mounding up the sand for the body when Ginny sensed someone standing behind her watching them. That wasn't at all unusual; they always attracted attention on the beach.

Suddenly, Beth turned her head and then jumped up and ran toward the person behind Ginny. "Hi, Grandpa!" she shouted.

Ginny stood up and turned around; she wanted to meet Beth's grandfather. She almost dropped the pen shell she'd been using to smooth the sand.

It was Nicholas.

He and Beth were hugging each other, her bare, sand-covered feet swimming in the air as he lifted her up in his arms and then set her down again. She ran back to her place and went back to work patting the mound into its proper shape.

Nicholas walked toward Ginny.

"Sorry, I didn't mean to interrupt things," he said.

"Beth is your granddaughter?"

"Yes. Isn't she wonderful? I talked to Marcy Monday night and mentioned what you were doing out here on the beach. She missed the article in the paper, and she knew Beth would love to join in. They live in Siesta Village, right behind the hardware store. Beth can walk over here."

"She has such artistic ability," Ginny said.

"We think so. And her mother tries to encourage it."

"That's good." Ginny always felt that adult encouragement meant so much in the development of any talent.

"I talked to Beth last night, and she was so excited about the castle you built yesterday that I had to come see what you're doing for myself," Nicholas said as he tried to pat his fly-away hair into place. In the constant sea breeze it was a losing battle.

"There are only remnants of the castle left," Ginny pointed to the now half destroyed walls and tower fifty feet away. "We build them near the high tide line so they are usually washed away by the next day or else we tear them down ourselves. We don't want the whole beach covered with the remains. But we couldn't quite bring ourselves to destroy yesterday's castle. It was special, and Beth should take a lot of credit for that."

"Would it disturb you if I stayed a while and watched?"

"No, of course not," she said, a little too eagerly she realized. "Perhaps I'll take a break and let the kids do this by themselves for a while. Beth seems to have things well under control."

Nicholas, dressed in shorts and one of his wildly colored Hawaiian shirts, had brought a low-slung beach chair which he unfolded. "Why don't you sit here?" he asked her.

"Thanks, but no. I have a beach towel." She picked up her folded towel and spread it out on the sand beside his chair. She opened her bottle of sun block and rubbed more on her legs and arms unnecessarily, mainly because she didn't know what to say to him. She felt exactly as she had in the ninth grade when a boy she'd admired from afar asked if he could sit beside her in the cafeteria. She'd wanted desperately to talk to him, but he was shy, too, and everything she thought of to say seemed too silly or unimportant.

So they sat silently throughout the whole lunch period, the only noise the rattle of their lunch sacks. As she chewed on her crisp carrot sticks, the sound seemed amplified a dozen times over in her head, and she was certain the whole room was listening to her chew. She'd been mortified.

She hadn't had that much trouble talking with Nicholas on

147

Monday. But the fact that he'd been on her mind so much since then disturbed her, and she felt embarrassed and ill at ease, fearful that he was somehow aware of her preoccupation.

Even Nicholas seemed to be short on words. He sat tracing circles in the sand with his forefinger, watching the children.

Finally Ginny said, "Have you found a judge yet?"

"Judge?"

"For the book of poetry."

"Oh . . . no. I've got some names to call but I haven't done it yet."

Ginny laughed. "I haven't gotten to the printers either. Naomi's going to fire us."

He smiled, evidently relieved. "Well, we'd better get on the stick, hadn't we? We ought to have something for them tomorrow."

"Tomorrow! Oh, Lord that's right. It's so easy to lose track of the days down here. I never seem to know what day it is."

"That's the whole idea, isn't it?"

"Mmmmm, maybe so. But I don't want to get completely out of sync. I need a little order in my life, but some days I feel like I'm losing it."

"I know the feeling." He said it with great seriousness and Ginny studied his face, trying to fathom the meaning behind his solemnity. But his features were as serene as usual.

Beth came over to her grandfather, shielding the sun from her eyes. "Grandpa, why don't you come help us?"

He turned to Ginny and grinned, and then said to Beth, "Why not? Your granddad isn't much of an artist, but I'd like to help."

Beth took his hand, and they walked over to the sand sculpture and sat down side-by-side. Ginny followed behind them and sat down on the far side of the mounded sand.

Nicholas joined in with great enthusiasm, if not skill. The

children had the rough form of the mermaid, but the finer features still needed to be worked on. Nicholas used a stick to draw scales on the long fish tail, while Beth worked on the face. She did a very creditable job of shaping the eyes, nose and mouth. Ginny smoothed the shoulder and neck methodically while watching the other two at work. She could see a great deal of resemblance between grandfather and granddaughter, and both had the same good-natured disposition.

It was soon time for Ginny to get dinner as the final touches on the sculpture were completed. Nicholas told Beth he'd give her a lift home, and she went to wash off her tools in the surf.

"That was the most refreshing afternoon I've had in a long, long time," he said to Ginny. "Would you mind if I join you now and then? Beth seemed to enjoy having me here."

"Of course not. Why should I mind?" But, in fact, she was distressed. She wanted him there, and she didn't want him there.

"I'll see you tomorrow at lunch then."

"Yes, tomorrow. Well, I've got to run and get dinner." Grabbing her bucket of tools, she turned and walked hurriedly down the beach toward Tranquility Gardens. She was anything *but* tranquil, however.

Twenty-One

The next morning Ginny briefly considered skipping lunch at Ramon's. Naomi was counting on her to have some figures from printers, though, so she dressed early to visit several print shops before meeting them at noon. After all, she'd just been accepted into this group, and she wasn't going to give it up. She was going to have to deal with her confused feelings for Nicholas in a mature way; surely she could handle this like an adult.

She wanted to have at least three estimates, and it took considerable time to discuss the plans for the book with each printer, so she barely made it to the restaurant by noon.

Naomi, Lucy Turner, Rebecca Stein, John Hildebrand, and Nicholas were there when she arrived. They all greeted her warmly, and she took a seat between Lucy and Rebecca. She'd seen Rebecca only on the beach during the sand sculpture contest and wanted to get better acquainted. She learned that "Becca," as she wanted to be called, had not been in the state long, having come to Sarasota for a public relations job. She confided to Ginny that she was tired already of cranking out hype for the local builders and realtors and found solace in writing poetry.

"Maybe we poets are all closet environmentalists," she said, "but it's truly hard to see the wisdom and beauty of row after row of high rises along these magnificent beaches."

"I live in one," said Ginny, "and I couldn't agree with you more."

After they finished eating, Naomi brought the others up to date on the plans for the book. Nicholas suggested the names of two possible judges, and they settled on a poet who taught at Eckerd College in St. Pete. Then Ginny presented the figures she'd gotten that morning. Since they'd planned for only a small run, knowing full well that poetry does not sell well, they were able to come in for slightly less than the $100 they'd earned as prize money at the sand sculpture contest.

"I think we're in good shape," said Naomi, pleased with the plans. "Since Lucy offered to use the computer at school to type it up, we're saving a great deal by having camera-ready copy. Bless you, Lucy, and bless word processing."

They all laughed.

"The next order of business is our readings. Ginny has agreed to read us her first effort. Go to it, Ginny."

She did so with great trepidation. The words that had seemed lyrical and crystalline to her earlier sounded leaden and vague as she read them aloud. By the time she reached the end of the short piece, she wished she'd never come. Who did she think she was anyway, Emily Dickinson? She should stick to sand castles.

There was a frightening moment of silence while the poets collected their thoughts.

"That's an intriguing notion," Lucy spoke first. "I would never have thought of comparing seaweed, of all things, to our own lives, but I think it works."

"I do, too," John tapped his pencil thoughtfully on the table as he studied the notes he'd made. "You've drawn an interesting parallel between man and nature that is quite unique. You have a few rough spots with your meter, but otherwise I think it's commendable."

Ginny felt so relieved they weren't trashing her effort, she could have cried. Then she remembered. "I've got to give Naomi some credit for this," she admitted. "She helped me a lot."

"The idea was all yours," Naomi acknowledged. "Very little of that is mine. I hope you'll go on now and write a lot more."

"I'll try." She felt as though she'd just passed a test, and had come out of it with at least a B, maybe a B plus. Why was it that everything seemed to remind her of her school days lately? Was it that things never really change, that life is a series of parallel experiences that happen over and over, forever putting one through trials that resonate with past events and emotions? That was why acceptance here meant so much to her, she realized. They had reaffirmed her faith in herself. She knew she would never be much of a poet, but belonging to this group was vital to her now, just as she'd needed to belong to a group when she was in junior high.

They discussed poems by Becca and John and ended the meeting by agreeing they would all contribute as many poems as possible for consideration in their book.

As the group started to gather up their things and leave, Nicholas came over to Ginny. "Could I take another look at your poem?" he asked.

"Sure," she said, handing it to him.

"I was wondering about your fourth line: 'yet scarcely moving.' It seems short. I thought maybe you could add a couple more beats like 'from its spot.' Something like that."

She nodded. "I'll take it under advisement." She didn't like the idea at all.

He continued to study the page. "You have very interesting handwriting," he said.

"Oh?"

"Yes, look at the loops on your g's and y's. And the way you cross your t's."

"Are you into graphology or something?"

"I've been interested in it for a long time, and I'm fairly

expert at it. I've even been asked by police on occasion to compare handwriting samples."

Ginny had always been intrigued by handwriting analysis and thought it would be fun to have hers evaluated. She wasn't sure she wanted it to be Nicholas who did it though.

"Have you got a minute?" he asked her. "I'll go over it and tell you what I see in it."

He apparently already had dissected her character while reading her poem. She might as well know what he found there.

"Sure. You've aroused my curiosity now." Ginny said. She'd meant to sound a little more enthusiastic but couldn't quite make it as her apprehension won out.

"I don't see why we can't stay here and have another cup of coffee. Ramon doesn't seem to need this table." He pulled out her chair for her and sat down beside her. The others had drifted off.

He studied the page seriously for several moments without speaking.

She felt uneasy; what secrets had she unwittingly revealed about herself in those few words?

"I'd say it reconfirms what I've thought about you," he said finally.

"Which is?"

"Well, for one thing you can cope. Whatever happens, you can always manage to pull yourself together by relying on inner strengths."

Ginny stared into her coffee cup. This was embarrassing, but fascinating, too.

"And see your straight lines and long 't' crossings. That means you stick with everything you undertake until you have seen it through. Other people learn to rely on you because of this."

"Oh, I'm not so sure . . ."

"Handwriting does not lie," he said firmly. "It also shows signs of family conditioning."

"What on earth is that?"

"It can mean family pride or it can mean over involvement with family; it's impossible to say which. But when it's this obvious, it means you should analyze yourself in relation to your family so that you will not confuse love for them with emotional dependence."

He glanced at her, she was sure to assess her reaction, though she was trying very hard not to show any reaction at all. "Please understand I am not making judgments of my own. I'm simply reading what your handwriting says. Think of it as scientific, which it is." Maybe he was having second thoughts about telling her this, too.

She wanted to call it off, but she didn't know how to do it without being ungracious. The best she could do was to pretend it was all in fun and she didn't believe any of it for a moment.

"Ummm," he continued, lowering his voice slightly, "the heavy pressure of your pen shows you are passionate."

She couldn't help but blush, although she thought this was absolutely wrong.

"You have vitality and a good capacity for work. You always carry through any task you are given."

"You mean I clean my house and get the meals like a good girl?"

"Come on, Ginny, this is serious. You are frank and sincere although sometimes you can be a little too frank. This is evident because you have few covering loops in the middle zone."

She had no idea what he was talking about. "Never. I'm the soul of tact."

He glanced at her quizzically and said nothing.

"Well, go on," she said.

"You might not like this one."

"You just told me I could cope. Let's hear it."

"The fact that your lines slant down at the end shows you have a tendency toward depression because you feel with more intensity than most people do. If you could express your feelings better and more often, you could fight it."

"Maybe I need to express my feelings in poetry. I'll have to admit I have a problem there. Is there anything else? Let me brace myself."

"One more thing, and it's good. You have a spirit of initiative. When you run into a difficult situation with no apparent solution, you work to find original answers. This helps you solve the problems in your life."

It was scary and funny and awesome all at once that he'd managed to plumb the depths of her so knowingly by looking at her handwriting. He'd told her things she knew about herself already. And there were some things she hoped were true, like having the initiative to solve problems, although she wasn't certain about that. One thing for sure, though, she was not going to even think about his comment on 'family conditioning.' There was too much emotional baggage tied up with that. And it frightened her that Nicholas seemed to know more about her than Leland did after thirty-eight years of marriage, at least more than he ever let on.

"Well," she said, "you leave me speechless."

"I didn't mean to do that, Ginny. I just think it's damn interesting what handwriting can say about a person. I found that my own was a revelation when I analyzed it."

She was very curious about what his revealed, but she didn't want him to know how interested she was, so she didn't ask.

He seemed to be lingering over his coffee as if waiting for her to say something, do something.

So she did. "I must be getting home now," she said. He

looked disappointed. "The children will be expecting me on the beach."

His appearance brightened considerably then. "I'd almost forgotten," he smiled. "I told Beth I would try to get there this afternoon."

Liar, she thought. She couldn't discourage him. It was, after all, a public place.

They each went their separate ways, but Ginny knew she would see him shortly on the beach. What could she do? She wasn't going to give up her afternoon sessions with the children just because Nicholas was there, too. If she were as frank as he had just told her she was, she'd tell him he made her nervous. But what the handwriting must not have revealed was that she was cowardly, too.

That night she called Melba; she felt a great need to talk to her.

"What's happening in Columbus?"

"Not much at all. When are you coming up? I miss you terribly."

"I can't come up there," she answered. "I'm kind of confused and depressed right now. Like I told you last time, if I came up, I'd feel like I had to go see the house. Why don't you come down?"

"Hon, I want to see you in the worst way. But Mickey is getting more crotchety by the day in his old age, and putting him in a kennel would probably kill him. I know his days are numbered, and he's meant so much to me, I just can't go off and leave him now."

"Whoever thought we'd let dogs and houses keep us apart."

"Whatever are you depressed about, Ginny?"

"I don't know. Can you get depressed by too much sunshine? Sometimes I long for a cold, lousy day just for the sake of variety. Leland's gone all day golfing or fishing. I suppose I should be thankful he's not underfoot all the time, but we seem to have very little to talk about now since I can't get the slightest bit interested in what he's doing. It was far more interesting when he was selling rubber products, believe it or not."

"Can't you find a niche of your own?"

"I have—sort of. The irony is that I haven't even told Leland about it."

"Why not, for heaven's sake?"

"Constance introduced me to this woman who talked me into joining this group of poets. But I'm so afraid Leland would make fun of them."

Melba sighed. "I see your point. I do know how Leland can be. Have you actually started to write poetry?"

Ginny laughed. "A grand total of one, and someone helped me with that one. But I plan to do more. And I do enjoy the people in the group."

"I think that's great. It's not my thing, but I admire anybody who tries to do it. Well, I do wish you'd change your mind about coming up. If you are really sick of sunshine, we have some wonderful shitty weather for you."

"Melba!"

"Don't be such an old maid, Ginny. Love ya!" And she hung up.

That's exactly what she was—an old maid, in spirit if not in reality. Could she ever change?

Leland was watching the stock market report when she returned to the living room.

"I talked with Melba," she said.

"How is the old girl?" he asked pleasantly.

"Damn it, Leland, we're not old. Don't say that."

"Sorry." He looked astonished. "What's with you?"

"Maybe I need a vacation. Can't we go somewhere?"

"A vacation? We are living a vacation. Where could we go

that's better? Why don't you go see Melba?"

He'd love to get rid of me, she thought. "She asked me to come, but the weather is terrible, and I don't want to see our burned down house."

"Don't go over there then."

"I'd have to visit the neighbors, and, besides, I'm sure I'd feel compelled to see it."

"I don't know what to tell you then," he sounded as if he was out of patience. "You'll have to work it out for yourself. Why don't you join a group—get involved in something besides playing in the sand."

She was so angry now she didn't care what she said. "I already have. That lunch I go to on Thursdays is really a group of poets."

"Poets?"

She tried to analyze the tone of his voice without success.

"Yes, Naomi invited me to meet with them, and she is helping me to write some poetry."

"Well, that sounds about on par with building sand castles."

She felt dizzy with anger and hurt, while at the same time she was aware that her emotions were all out of proportion to the moment. "Fuck you, Leland!" She screamed at the top of her lungs.

Words she had never before uttered. She ran into the bedroom, slammed the door, and fell sobbing onto the bed. Nor did the irony of the fact that she was lying upon their wedding ring quilt escape her.

Twenty-Two

Fifteen minutes later Leland tapped on the bedroom door.

"Come in," she called, her voice catching with emotion. She wiped her eyes on the hem of her skirt.

He opened the door and came in slowly. "Well," he said, his arms dangling awkwardly at his sides. "Have you worked it through yet?"

"I don't know," she sniffed.

"I was making a joke, Ginny. I guess I was a little insensitive, but I never expected such a violent reaction. What on earth is eating you?"

She rolled over on her back and gazed at him, nudging tears from the corners of her eyes with the sides of her hands. "I'm not sure. A little bit of everything. Tranquility Gardens . . . you making fun of the things I do . . . the damn sun shining day after day after day. I just can't seem to make the adjustment."

"You don't like the sunshine . . . ?" His voice was incredulous.

"Oh, that's just indicative of the unreality of this place. In real life the sun doesn't shine every day."

Leland's face showed his inward struggle between sympathy and impatience. Impatience won out. "That's the silliest thing I ever heard."

She rolled back over on her stomach and lay with her eyes closed, her head cradled in the crook of her arm. She was going to ignore him, shut him out. Maybe she could manage to sleep and not have to think about anything.

Leland sat down on the bed beside her, his hand on her back.

"I'm sorry, Ginny," he said. "I seem to have the habit of sticking my foot in my mouth."

She didn't answer.

"I'm having such a good time here, I guess I can't accept the fact that you aren't. Give it time. I promise to keep my mouth shut about the sand castles and poetry."

She was pretty sure the condescension she heard was not all in her mind, but she still didn't move or speak.

He sat for a few minutes waiting for her to respond, but when she didn't, he finally left the room.

She fell asleep not long after that and never heard Leland come to bed. The next morning they both pretended that nothing had happened the night before.

But Ginny could feel an invisible barrier inside her, a barrier raised to resist the barbs Leland might toss off in spite of his vow. He was true to his word, though. He never spoke of her castle building or poetry again. It was as if the most important parts of her life didn't exist as far as he was concerned.

Nicholas was now showing up at the beach several times a week. At first he felt compelled to say that Beth had asked him to come, but after a while he apparently felt he no longer needed an excuse. Sometimes they would work with the children, sometimes they would merely sit and watch, giving them words of encouragement or advice now and then. These were the times they would have long conversations.

Nicholas was easy to talk to. And they talked about many things—their lives before Florida, their children, his grandchildren. She even told to him about Donald's problems as a teenager, how they agonized over his involvement with drugs. In a way it had drawn Leland and her closer together, she told Nicholas, in their desperation and determination to "save" him.

(At least she'd thought that at the time. Now she wondered if that was true since she'd learned of his infidelity.) They finally decided to send Donald to a special school that specialized in tough love. When he came out of there he seemed at first sullen. He didn't want to go to college in spite of his ability. But a year pumping gas changed his attitude completely, and he gladly went off to school. He'd been on a successful track ever since, though Ginny worried about him working too hard. She always wondered if he was subconsciously trying to compensate for the unhappiness he'd caused them.

Nicholas told her about his wife Trudy, and how acutely he'd missed her, though as he said, time took away the sharpness of the pain. He didn't mention her over and over, though, as did some widowers, who constantly spoke of their deceased spouses as if afraid they would totally fade from memory if not resurrected daily in their conversations.

Ginny talked about Leland on occasion, but she always was careful to present him in a benign manner. She could never confess her unhappiness to Nicholas. Maybe it was that "family conditioning" he'd spoken of when he analyzed her handwriting, but she always kept her marital problems to herself. Melba, of course, was the one exception. She had a couple of times expressed her frustrations to her sister. Not that she ever got much sympathy.

Nicholas, though, was full of surprises. One day he showed up with half a dozen miniature flags made from dowels and scraps of brilliant fabric.

"All good castles should have flags," he said, planting them on the towers of that day's building. "We need some color out here." From then on, every castle was decorated with at least one or two pennants. And every day when they checked the remnants of yesterday's efforts, they were gone, a small treasure picked up by an anonymous beachcomber.

"You can't continue to bring flags all the time," Ginny told him. "That's a lot of trouble, and somebody usually rips them off."

"That's the idea," he smiled. "They're souvenirs for kids who visit the beach, something they can take home to remember the day. They're nothing to make, and I'm glad someone wants them."

"You're always so thoughtful, Nicholas," she said.

Ginny was attempting to write more poems, and Nicholas would read and discuss them with her. He was a better critic than he was a poet, and generally he could sense when a word or phrase wasn't right, especially when it was in someone else's poem. She wondered why that was so and decided he was too emotionally involved in his own poetry to see it objectively.

"I've been working on a poem about sandpipers," she said one day. "I'm fascinated by them. Do you ever notice how they all face into the wind together? They act like they're all activated by the same switch."

"Next to watching pelicans dive for fish, I'd rather watch those little guys. Let me hear your poem."

"I think you need to see it instead. I wrote it on the paper so it looks like a sandpiper running back and forth."

She handed him a folded sheet from her bag.

SANDPIPERS

A score or more scurry
along the sand,
puppet-birds pulled
by invisible strings,
reverse direction
on silent command,
uncannily in unison.
Bird-dancers

balance on delicate legs
rehearsing the steps
of a seashore ballet
performed to the song
of the surf.

He studied it quite a few minutes in spite of its brevity.

"I like it a lot. I wouldn't change a thing."

"Really?"

"Really. And I hope you submit it for the book. We only have three more weeks to get them in, remember. How many have you written?"

"Only five or six I'd show anybody. A lot of junk I've thrown out."

"I think you judge them too harshly. I haven't seen anything bad yet."

"That's because I won't show you the bad ones." She winked at him.

Suddenly she fell silent as feelings of . . . was it guilt, or longing, or what? . . . coursed through her. This was the kind of easy banter she should be sharing with Leland. These were the moments she wanted to share with him, not someone else. She was crazy to put herself in such a vulnerable position by seeing Nicholas here on the beach so often. But what was she supposed to do, lock herself in her room? No, she was an adult. She could keep herself on an even keel.

Nicholas, always intuitive of her moods, sat quietly, rereading her poem. His white hair fluttered about his head in the breeze like the tiny flags on the castle towers. His dark glasses hid any clue to what he was thinking that could be revealed in his eyes. He wore bathing trunks and his shirtless torso had become deep bronze from the many afternoons they'd shared in the sun. The silvery hair on his chest glistened against the tan like the old fashioned angel's hair they'd used on their Christmas tree when she was a child. The same sweet odor of aftershave hung about him even here. The only motion that he made was the gentle stroking of the paper to smooth it as he read the poem silently. He might as well have been stroking her.

My God, did this man do these things knowingly? He always maintained such an innocent air she could never be sure. He was either one of the wiliest men she'd ever known, or the most ingenuous.

In late May, the final day they were to submit their poems for the book, Nicholas asked her to stay after their luncheon meeting. More attended than usual, there were nine in all present, probably drawn by the possibility of getting into print, a feat not easily accomplished by poets. There were a couple of people there Ginny had never met.

"Just mention the word 'publish' and they come out of the woodwork," Naomi whispered to her. "But ask them to do some work on the book, and they'll just as quickly disappear."

The meeting was extra long as some final details were decided upon, and it was after two before they adjourned, each handing Nicholas his or her submission on the way out.

"Could you stay a few minutes and help me with this?" he called across the large table as Ginny got ready to leave.

"Sure," she said, wondering what he wanted her to do.

He wordlessly patted and juggled the pile of papers into one neat stack as the others lingered about the table in last minute farewells. She could sense he was waiting for them all to leave before he spoke, so she finally sat down beside him to wait. Five minutes later the last stragglers left.

"Do you have some time?" he asked.

"Yes. The children have been doing so well working while we talk, they'd probably not miss us if we didn't show up at all."

"I like the way you said 'we,' as if we were a pair."

Her alarm system, sensitive as a smoke alarm, was clanging in her head. She didn't know what to say, so she was silent.

"It's taken me a long time to work up the nerve for this," he said looking at her with an intensity quite unlike his usual placid manner.

She edged herself slightly away from him. "Something tells me I don't want to hear this, Nicholas."

"Please," he said, putting his hand on her forearm gently, but firmly, as if he had no intention of letting her leave. "Hear me out."

She blew out her breath in what sounded like a sigh but was in fact an attempt to steady her emotions. "Okay, say it." She sounded grim, but it was unintentional.

"We've spent a lot of time together these past few weeks, and I don't know about you, but I've felt more relaxed and happy with you than I have with anyone since my wife died."

He searched her face waiting for her reply. When she said nothing, he continued.

"It's been on my mind constantly lately, the fact that I get a very strong sense that things aren't right between you and Leland. All sorts of signs make me sure that it's so, Ginny. You can't deny it, can you?"

She instinctively put her hand to her mouth as if holding back words she never said, ashamed to think she'd let an outsider glimpse into the privacy of her relationship with Leland. He must have deduced things from casual comments, or her mood swings, or perhaps even her handwriting. God, she felt terrible that he had so easily identified her problem.

"I don't want to talk about it," she said, afraid he was going to question her.

"Of course not. I'm sure it's too painful. What I'm trying to say, and I'm not doing a very good job at it, is that I would like to try and make your life happier. I think I could do it; I think

165

our relationship is very special."

Oh my God, she should have realized that Nicholas, too much of a gentleman to make a sexual advance like stealing a kiss or simply coming on to her (she still was sure the knee incident at Naomi's had been perfectly innocent), was going to ask her in a roundabout way if she wanted to have an affair. She couldn't deny that the thought had entered her mind before now.

She had long ago decided that she could never manage it. Maybe all the heroines in the novels and movies didn't think twice about infidelity, but she either grew up in the wrong age or the wrong family because she couldn't conceive of being able to handle it emotionally. She was sure she would be destroyed by the guilt and fear of being found out. She had much greater capacity for dealing with unhappiness and the lack of communication with Leland than sustaining a secret romance. It was out of the question.

"Stop right there, Nicholas. You're a wonderful person and I've enjoyed these afternoons more than you'll ever know, but it just isn't in me to have an affair."

He grabbed her hand in his. "Oh, no, no, you misunderstand. I don't want an affair. I could never settle for having you on a part-time basis. What I meant was I want to marry you!" His voice had begun to rise, and Ginny looked around in alarm to make sure no one heard him. The only other couple still in the restaurant was deep in their own conversation and paid no attention to them.

She jerked her hand from his. "I've been married for thirty-eight years," she said, unconsciously twisting the wedding band back and forth on her finger. "You don't just walk out on someone after thirty-eight years."

He looked down like a chastened child, but then continued his earnest plea. "Sometimes people grow in different directions; it happens all the time. You have another twenty or thirty years left at least. Are you willing to be miserable all that time? Should you sacrifice your happiness for the rest of your life for a commitment made when you were practically a child?" He stopped for a minute as though working up the courage to continue.

"I'm sorry if I sound like I'm quoting from some 'how-to-leave-your-spouse-and-be-happy' book. My motives are selfish, of course, because I know how happy you would make me. I think we could have a wonderful life together. Think about it, Ginny. Think about the good times we could have."

She was stunned. As she tried to analyze her feelings, it came to her with a devastating impact: she'd wanted Nicholas to propose an affair, which she would of course turn down, because she needed the assurance that she was desirable and attractive. She'd never considered, though, the price they both would have to pay: Nicholas would lose his own self esteem when she refused him, and she probably would no longer have the daily companionship that he gave her.

But this was something else entirely. In all her unhappiness these past few months, never once had she thought of leaving Leland. That option was so foreign to her thinking that she'd not even considered it. But maybe her outlook was too circumscribed, too old fashioned. A third or more of the population did more than consider it, they acted upon it. Wasn't it ultimately more honorable and honest to divorce your mate and marry another than to carry on a secret liaison behind your husband's back? She could at least think about it, couldn't she?

"Oh, Nicholas, I never expected anything like this. I don't know what to say. My first impulse is to say let's pretend this never happened."

"And your second impulse?" He looked at her with the question lingering in his eyes.

"I've got a lot of thinking to do. Never in my wildest imagination did I ever dream I would even consider such a thing."

"That's why I'm so crazy about you, Ginny. Your loyalty to Leland under impossible circumstances is one of your best virtues. I saw it in your handwriting. I also saw the fact that you can confuse love with emotional dependence. Isn't that really what you have with Leland? Aren't you kidding yourself that what you feel for him is honest-to-God love?"

What could she say? She didn't know anymore what she felt for Leland. Her emotions were such a muddled mess she wasn't sure she could ever sort them out.

"I can't promise anything, Nicholas, except that I'll think about it. But please, don't get your hopes up."

"That's all I can ask for, Ginny. Just give me a chance."

"I need time, though. And I think it would be best if we don't see each other on the beach in the meantime. I don't want to miss the Thursday lunches, but I'd appreciate it if you didn't come to the beach for a while."

"Whatever you say. I'll do anything if there is the slightest chance that you would marry me." He took her hand, held it tightly for a minute, then raised it to his lips and barely brushed it with a kiss.

How like him, Ginny thought; gallantry does not die. But was he, in fact, her knight in shining armor?

Twenty-Three

Ginny felt as if she'd been cut adrift in a tiny raft in the vast emptiness of the ocean and was paddling frantically to find land. But what kind of land was she looking for? Did she seek the familiar shape of her past life, the marriage in which she had invested so many years, and which, until recently, she'd considered as happy as anyone could reasonably expect? Had the turning point been when she learned of Leland's affair? Or was it the move to Florida where she felt so strange, so foreign somehow. If it weren't for the poetry group, she would be even more discontented than she was. And Leland either didn't realize, or didn't care, about the extent of her frustration. He was too busy having a good time.

Or was she looking for new territory, where she could be with someone who appreciated her talents, modest as they were, and could encourage her search for identity.

Yes, that was it. She didn't know who she was, and she was sixty years old! But Nicholas constantly gave her parameters she could measure herself by. When he discussed her poetry, analyzed her handwriting, even in the building of sand castles he was helping her to define herself.

She was scared. She'd never before been faced with such a wrenching decision. She'd always been pulled along by life, going wherever it took her. She'd never dated anyone but Leland; their marriage had seemed inevitable. Just as her whole life had been inevitable.

That hadn't seemed bad before, in fact it seemed good. She'd always considered herself one of the lucky ones for whom everything fell into place. It was only during these past few months that she'd felt unease and doubt. Did she in fact always take the easy way out? Should she have taken a more active role in determining her life's direction? The magazines kept exhorting women to be assertive. But what little assertiveness she'd attempted recently was met with indifference or incomprehension.

So now she had an important choice to make for her future. Oh, God, did she have a choice, and she found she didn't want one.

It was hard to act normal with Leland when her mind was in such turmoil. But either she was a very good actress or he was so unobservant that he seemed to be totally unaware. Anyone with half an eye could see she was a mass of nerves.

And so the next couple of weeks passed while she was caught in a state of panic, gripped by a complete inability to make a decision. Any decision. When Leland asked her if she wanted to go out to dinner, she could only shrug and say it was up to him. She had difficulty deciding what to cook, and it even extended to what to wear each day. Out on the beach in the afternoons, she sat in a state of limbo letting the children work without her. They asked her to come help, but the inertia was too great, and she would sit on a beach towel, listlessly sifting sand through her fingers.

When she went to the Thursday luncheons, Nicholas would sit across from her, saying nothing to her directly but trying to catch her eye. She was acutely aware of him watching her and tried not to meet his gaze. Sometimes, of course, their eyes would meet briefly, and it was as if an electric current jolted through her. He was being very patient. He had not contacted her at all since that day, but she could tell from his glance that he wanted her answer. The right one. And soon.

It was in the third week of her indecision that Leland told her about the trip. He was very excited about it.

"Pat Patterson's taking a group of us down to the Keys for a five-day fishing trip. Apparently he does this annually, and everybody wants to go along. So I feel real flattered that he asked me."

"When is this?" she felt she almost asked him too quickly.

"We leave next Monday. You'll be okay won't you?"

"Sure, I'll be fine." But she didn't think she'd be fine at all. If Leland left, she wasn't sure what she'd do. She knew how lonely she always became when Leland left town. She hated evenings most of all; there was something about nighttime that intensified her loneliness. The next morning, as soon as Leland had left for his golf game, she called Melba.

"I need you to come down here next week," she began without any pleasantries.

"Hon, I'd love to but you know I can't on account of Mickey."

"Look, this is an emergency. Bring Mickey with you."

"I thought you weren't allowed to have dogs in your condo."

"We're not, but we'll sneak him in. Everybody near us is gone or is so deaf they'll never know the difference."

"What's the matter, Ginny?"

"I can't tell you now. I'll explain it when you get here. But, please Melba believe me, I need you."

"Well, let me see if I can get a flight and I'll call you back."

"You'll save my life."

Melba called back within the hour and told Ginny she'd be in at 9:30 Sunday evening. "I hope poor Mickey can handle it. He's never flown before," she said.

"He'll be fine. I'm just going to tell Leland you're coming to keep me company while he's gone. He's going on a fishing trip to the Keys for five days."

"Is that the emergency, you don't want to be alone?" Melba sounded a little annoyed.

"No, it's more than that."

"Good Lord, I'll go crazy wondering what it's all about."

"Sorry, Melba."

"Be that way. I'll see you Sunday night then." Her sister's voice had softened, and she sounded almost sympathetic.

When Ginny hung up, she decided that Melba would not only have to save her from doing something foolish in a fit of loneliness, the main reason she'd called her, but she'd also have to help her decide what to do with her life. She'd always admired her sister's ability to make tough decisions, and she'd acted with courage and strength throughout her husband Mack's terminal illness. Maybe her handwriting showed initiative, but she couldn't conjure up an ounce of it at this point.

Leland and Ginny met Melba at the airport Sunday night. She was concerned because the flight had been rough over Georgia, and she wasn't sure how Mickey had made out.

"Poor baby," she said, waiting for him to be brought from the cargo hold. "He's probably scared to death." Ginny could never understand Melba's maternal fussing over a dog. She thought it incongruous that a woman who handled every other aspect of her life with such calm maturity could be reduced to baby talk over a scraggly mutt. But then Ginny had never lived alone, nor had a pet, so she probably wasn't the best one to judge.

Finally an attendant brought Mickey to the waiting group. He did look cowed, he even trembled a little, but when he spied Melba, he went crazy, barking and dancing about in a doggie St. Vitas' Dance.

"Oh, you poor darling," she crooned, leaning over and letting him out of his carrier. She picked him up, letting him lick her face. It was a small dog, a mixture of terrier and God-knows-what-else, but the terrier's yapping bark had survived the mixing, and Ginny was embarrassed as nearly everyone in the terminal turned to see what the commotion was.

"I hope to God he doesn't bark like that at the condo. They'll throw us all out," Ginny said in the car on the way home.

Melba nuzzled Mickey's head with her nose. He was perched on her lap. "He'll be quiet as a mouse. He only barks when we've been separated. He hates to be alone, just like you, Ginny." The last was surely meant as a dig.

It was nearly eleven when they reached Tranquility Gardens. Most of the lights were out.

"I don't think anyone will see us," Ginny told Melba. "But it might be a good idea if you carried Mickey instead of letting him walk. There'd be less chance of anyone noticing him that way."

So they walked triple file, Leland in front carrying the heaviest suitcase, Melba in the middle cradling Mickey in her arms, and Ginny bringing up the rear with a small bag. But the human shield was unnecessary. No one passed or saw them on the way to their condo.

When they entered the living room, Melba set Mickey down and took in a sharp breath. "This is gorgeous. You guys are really living dangerously with all this white carpet, aren't you?"

Leland laughed. "Everyone down here has white I think. There's no dirt to track in, only sand. At least, that's the theory. They sort of forgot about the blacktop on the parking lot which gets on your shoes and tracks in. Anyway, let me show you your room."

They took her luggage to the guest bedroom and then gave her a tour of the house.

"Wait till tomorrow when the sun's up," said Leland. "The view will knock your socks off."

"I can't wait," Melba answered.

"Well, I don't know about you two, but I've got to be up and about by six so I'm going to bed." Leland was to meet Pat in the parking lot at seven to ride with him to the downtown marina where Pat kept his boat. "Sleep in, Melba. I'll sneak out quietly."

"Okay, Leland, have a great trip and catch a bunch."

"Don't say that!" Ginny pressed the back of her hand to her forehead in mock horror. "We've got enough fish in the freezer for the next five years already. I've told him to throw them all back."

"Well, shoot, can't you pack them in dry ice and let me take some home?" Melba asked them.

"I don't know why not. See there, Ginny, someone appreciates my fishing skills," Leland gloated.

"I thought they just jumped in the boat, that it didn't take talent." Ginny realized there was an edge to her voice that she hadn't meant to put there, although she was thinking you don't appreciate my talents, why should I appreciate yours?

"Goodnight ladies." Leland ignored her sarcasm and went into the bedroom.

Melba looked at Ginny, her eyes questioning, but she said nothing.

"Look," said Ginny, "it's late and I know you're tired. Let's go to bed and talk tomorrow. Okay?"

"Sure." Melba gave her sister a lingering hug.

Ginny had purchased a dog bed for Mickey, and they padded it with an old beach towel and put it beside Melba's bed. The dog, exhausted from the trip and the trauma of being separated from Melba, climbed wearily into it and fell asleep almost immediately.

Ginny was not so lucky, though. She lay awake for hours, wondering if she had done the right thing by asking Melba to come.

TWENTY-FOUR

Ginny had been asleep only a short while when the alarm went off. Leland got up immediately and went to shower, eager to leave. She fixed him a substantial breakfast, but had difficulty eating much because her stomach felt so queasy. If she hadn't known better, she would have thought she was in the throes of a flu siege. But it was nothing but sheer nerves, unlike anything she'd experienced before. Ginny still couldn't believe she'd managed to get herself into such an incredible predicament.

The most difficult decision she'd had to make before this was in the realm of whether to have turkey or ham for Christmas. Of course there had been the move to Florida, but Leland, in reality, had made that decision and she'd gone meekly along as always.

As soon as Leland left, Melba came into the kitchen in her robe. Ginny was sitting at the table, staring out at the parking lot. The sky was rosy with morning light, and she watched Leland ride off toward town. As the car disappeared from sight on Midnight Pass Road, she wanted to weep. She hated him for abandoning her now, leaving her so vulnerable, even if he didn't have the slightest inkling of her dilemma.

"I just looked out your living room windows," Melba greeted her. "I can't believe that view. It's incredible."

Ginny nodded without being able to muster a smile.

Melba poured herself a cup of coffee and sat down opposite

her. "What's wrong, Ginny? Something terrible is eating at you, I can tell."

Ginny put some sweetener in her coffee and then stirred and stirred long after it had dissolved. "I don't know where to start."

"How about at the beginning?" Melba asked, looking at her squarely.

"It's this place, Melba. Everyone thinks this place is so wonderful, and I'll admit the view is nice and all that, but most of our neighbors are a lot older, and I have so little in common with them. The worst part is that they don't let children live here so it's like being in an old folks' home all the time."

"You're free to come and go, aren't you? You're not chained to the wall, after all."

"I do go out. I have to. I started making sand castles with the kids on the beach. I haven't told you this, but Donald and Susan have decided not to have children, so these kids are my substitute grandkids."

"Well, I'm not surprised that Susan made that decision. But I'm shocked Donald goes along with it," Melba said.

"He goes along with anything she wants. He doesn't like to rock the boat."

"Yeah, I suppose he does. Anyway, with the kids on the beach you can enjoy them, but you don't have to worry about them."

"It's not the same though. I want grandchildren in the worst way, but I'm not going to make myself sick over the fact I can't have them."

"I should hope not."

"Anyway, one day a news photographer took my picture with these kids building a sand castle and it was in our local newspaper. Leland made some snide remark. Said he would get razzed by his golf buddies."

Melba made a wry smile. "Leland can be a prick at times. But you've known that and have lived with it for a long time.

Why does it bug you now?"

Ginny sipped her coffee and gazed at Melba's sleep-tousled hair. Her sister was always so particular about how she looked that she seldom appeared even slightly unkempt, even at a time like this. But stranger yet was her attitude. Melba, who was usually her strongest ally, seemed unmoved by her complaints. In fact it seemed as though she was challenging her unhappiness.

"I guess too much has happened this year. The accident and finding out about Leland's affair and the move and learning that our old house burned all rolled together has made me a little crazy. I can't cope anymore."

Melba patted Ginny's hand like a teacher encouraging a student who'd just flunked an exam. "It's been a rough year for you, there's no denying that. But you're tougher than you realize, Ginny. I'm sure with time things will get back to normal."

"I haven't told you everything yet. There's more to it." Ginny's stomach was wracked by sharp pains now, and she vowed again to give up coffee, a vow she knew she'd never be able to keep.

Melba looked wary, as if she could sense what was coming. "I had a hunch. You didn't drag me down here just to tell me Leland said you were undignified."

Ginny ignored that. "When Constance was here in January, she introduced me to a woman who's a poet as I told you on the phone. Did you know Constance wrote poetry?"

Melba shook her head no. "She can never get a word in edgewise with Wally around. Who does know what the girl can do?"

"I felt like I hardly knew her either. But she's quite a gal in her own quiet way. But anyway, I like this Naomi, and she got me interested in writing poetry, too. I don't know if you remember that I wrote some when I was a teenager. I guess you were gone by then."

"I remember Mom mentioning it. She was terribly proud of you."

"You're kidding! I had no idea. You know how Mom was; she'd brag on you to everyone else, but she'd never tell you to your face that you'd done something good." Ginny thought again how she'd learned more about her mother since she died than she ever knew when she was alive. "Anyway, Naomi is in this group that meets for lunch every Thursday to read and critique each others' poetry. She asked me to join them."

"That's great, Ginny," Melba said. "That should make you feel like you have a stake in something."

"It means more to me than you know. But, of course, you can imagine what Leland thinks of it."

Melba could only shake her head with a half smile. She didn't need a diagram drawn. "Can I guess that he's made a snide remark or two about that also?"

"Only once. I refuse to discuss it any more because I know darn well what he'll say. 'You mean to tell me you spent all day writing eight lines of poetry? God, Ginny, can't you find anything better than that to do with your time?' " She mimicked perfectly Leland's voice and the way he pounced upon consonants as though attacking them when he became agitated.

Melba got up to pour herself another cup of coffee. "So to say you two aren't on the greatest terms right now is an understatement."

"On the surface we're quite cordial. But we don't really say anything to each other any more. We talk about the weather or the economy or his golf game. We never discuss my interests because he thinks they're trivial. It's as though we've just met and are making small talk."

"Why don't you force the issue, tell him how you feel."

"I have—several times. I've told him how unhappy I am, but he can't understand it at all, and he's sure I'll get over it. He thinks this place is paradise."

Melba held her coffee cup in front of her with both hands and stared vacantly into its depths as if looking for answers there.

"That's coffee, not tea leaves," Ginny said, trying to lighten the mood.

"What I'm wondering," Melba said, "is why you couldn't tell me this on the telephone. Not that I didn't want to see you and your place, but I don't understand the urgency."

Ginny bit her lip, her heart pounding, as she willed herself the courage to say it. She had to tell her, that was why she begged her to come, but it would set her on an irreversible course toward making a decision that she dreaded. "I want you to meet someone."

Melba looked at her sharply. "And . . . ?"

Ginny couldn't meet her eye. She folded and unfolded her napkin nervously. "I want you to meet a man who wants to marry me."

There was a stunned silence for a very long while.

"Marry you? Doesn't he know you're already married?"

"Yes, he wants me to leave Leland."

"I can't believe you're saying this. Who is he?"

"He belongs to the poetry group. He is the most gentle, kind and understanding man I've ever met."

"Really, Ginny, you sound like a bad romance novel."

"I can talk to him, Melba. He's interested in all the same things I am. We discuss poetry and how we feel about everything—which is more than I can do with Leland these days. He comes to the beach in the afternoons and helps me with the sand castles. His granddaughter lives here, and that's why he started working with me . . . for her sake."

"Oh, come on," said Melba, her expression one of total incredulity.

Ginny surprised herself by slamming the napkin onto the table. "Dammit, Melba, don't mock me. You've already made up your mind!" She couldn't remember raising her voice to her sister since they'd become adults.

Melba was taken aback by her outburst. "I guess I underestimated your feelings toward him," she said apologetically.

"I'm so mixed up right now I don't know what my feelings are." She dabbed at her eyes with the napkin as tears began to well in spite of her determination to stay calm. "That's why I needed you here, to help me sort things out. But, please, please, have an open mind, Melba. I've always looked up to you and valued your opinion. Try and see it from my point of view."

"Well," Melba shrugged, "what do you want me to do? Nobody else can make that kind of decision for you."

"I want you to meet him, get to know him. I can't seem to be objective right now . . . too many things have happened; I'm too upset with Leland. All I know is I can't face another thirty years feeling as miserable as I do right now. You've always had your act together, Melba. I would gladly listen to your advice. If you would promise to try and be unbiased when you talk to Nicholas and judge him for what he really is. Could you do that for me, please?"

Melba's features for the first time showed real compassion. "Oh, babe, all I can do is try. It's going to be the hardest thing I've ever done, but I'll do my damnedest. Just remember that I'm no oracle, so don't take what I say as if it were engraved in stone. It's your life, and you have to live it the best you can."

"I know that. But I still want your input. You're my best friend as well as my sister, and your opinion means more to me than anybody else's."

"Give what's-his-name a call then and set up a luncheon date. What did you say his name is?"

"Nicholas." Ginny got up and walked around the table. She

put her arms around Melba's shoulders and laid her cheek on top of her head. "I miss you terribly, you know. That was the worst part of moving out of Columbus."

Melba grasped her encircling arms tightly. "You couldn't feel worse than I do about it."

A strange scratching sound came from the foyer.

"Oh, Lord," Melba said, "that's Mickey. He has to go out. What do I do now?"

"Would you mind carrying him out? We could cover him with a beach towel, and there's a grove of palms down by the road. You could let him go down there."

Melba started to laugh. "Honest to God, Ginny, it's bad enough having to meet your lover without having to play undercover agent with Mickey."

"He is not my lover."

"Oh, sure," she grinned. "Whatever you say, hon."

"Well, don't believe me then, but it's true."

TWENTY-FIVE

Ginny knew that Nicholas got up early so she dialed his number while Melba took her shower. He answered on the second ring.

"This is Ginny."

"Ginny," he repeated with warmth and a note of expectation in his voice. "Does this mean you have something to tell me? I was beginning to be afraid I was never going to hear from you again."

"Not exactly. I'm having a lot of trouble with this, Nicholas. You'll have to bear with me."

"As long as you like." He sounded sincere.

"My sister, Melba, is in town, and I wanted you two to meet. Could we have lunch together today?"

"Just name the place."

"Anywhere but Ramon's, I don't want to run into anybody I know."

"Okay. How about that place on the Key, the one that looks like a greenhouse in the jungle?"

"You mean the Summerhouse."

"That's it. I'll pick you up at 12:30. Is it all right if I come to the condo?"

"Yes, Leland's out of town. We'll see you then, Nicholas."

At twelve-thirty exactly, the doorbell rang. Ginny opened the door and was relieved to see that Nicholas was wearing a conservative pale yellow sport shirt instead of his usual vibrant one. But his hair still had the flyaway look that she normally found endearing; now it seemed merely untidy. Melba had always been so fussy about Mack's appearance, and Ginny had noticed that even Leland gave his clothes and hair an extra once-over when they were going to see her sister. Melba had a way of noticing flaws and making one self-conscious about them. She would make a little ceremony of picking lint from a jacket or patting down a stray lock. She always looked immaculate herself, and even Ginny, who was reasonably particular about her appearance, felt less than perfectly groomed around her. What on earth was she going to think about Nicholas who was the epitome of sartorial indifference?

"Hi," he said shyly, like a teenager picking up a first date.

"Come on in." She hadn't realized how uncomfortable she would be in his presence. How could she possibly relax and be herself when so much was at stake? She fervently wished she'd never invited Melba down, arranged this lunch, or said she would even consider his proposal.

She introduced Melba to him and was certain she could detect disapproval in her manner although she was perfectly gracious as always. Nicholas would never sense it.

Out in the parking lot, as Melba climbed into the back seat of Nicholas' car, Ginny noticed her slight grimace as she moved books that were scattered across the seat.

"Oh, sorry," Nicholas said. "I keep meaning to return those to the library, but I keep forgetting." Forgetfulness was another trait that Melba disdained.

They arrived at the Summerhouse and parked in the shade of a live oak tree. The builders somehow had managed to save the tiny jungle that existed on this particular lot and had built an almost all-glass building in its midst. Seated inside, one could no longer see the high rises that dominated the landscape, and diners felt transported to some untamed island far from civilization.

They all ordered wine, and began to relax in the intimate atmosphere of their table which was tucked into a far corner, surrounded by the huge greenhouse-style windows that made them feel part of the outdoors.

"I understand that you and Ginny belong to a poetry group," Melba said languidly. She always mellowed rapidly under the influence of a single glass of wine. Ginny was aware of this and had ordered Chardonnay first although she seldom drank wine at noon. But she knew Melba undoubtedly would follow suit, and she preferred to have her tractable and receptive.

"Oh, yes. We have a small group that gets together regularly. We're no literary lights, but it gives us a chance to have our little say in a way that won't offend too many people. We hope," Nicholas added.

"Do you mean you don't offend many people because so few people read it?"

Nicholas laughed. "Touché. No, what I meant was that we can rant and rave, but when it's couched in poetic language, it seems more civilized, or should I say gentlemanly?"

"Oh, no," chortled Melba. "Do I detect a bit of chauvinism there?"

"Lord no," said Ginny. "Nicholas is the least chauvinistic man I know. I think he meant artful, didn't you, Nicholas?"

"Artful, subtle, whatever. Maybe we're just cowards about saying what we have to say straight out."

"But from what I understand, you're not a coward at all about speaking your mind," Melba said almost coquettishly.

Ginny kicked her sister under the table. She certainly didn't want to discuss Nicholas' proposal openly. She only wanted Melba to get to know him and be able to help her make some kind of intelligent decision about her life. She was beginning to regret the Chardonnay.

Nicholas acted as though he did not catch her meaning.

"Some of my poetry has been criticized as too didactic. I get so frustrated about environmental issues sometimes that I let 'em have it. But I get a lot of flack when I do."

Melba responded instantly to Ginny's kick and pulled herself erect in the chair. Her tone was suddenly serious. "This is my first trip to Florida, and I'm shocked at the building going on, especially along the beaches."

That was the very thing Nicholas needed to launch him on a long and emotional discourse on the plight of Florida. The conversation did not lag for the next hour and a half, and they were so engrossed that they were startled to find themselves the lone diners.

"Whoops," said Ginny, glancing around the room, "I think we've overstayed our welcome. We should be getting back. Melba wants to help me with the sand castles."

Nicholas had the sad look of a little boy. His eyes told volumes. "I really miss that, Ginny. Beth asked me the other day why I didn't come any more."

"Who's Beth?" Melba asked.

"My granddaughter. She's one of Ginny's groupies, if you will, and the reason I started going there."

Melba caught Ginny's eye momentarily.

Ginny merely stared back unflinchingly, unwilling to let on she'd understood. She decided it would be simply an extension of this luncheon if she asked Nicholas to join them.

"Oh, you might as well come on . . . today anyway," she said, emphasizing the today part.

They went back to the condo, and Ginny, with many misgivings, found a pair of Leland's swim trunks for Nicholas to wear so he wouldn't have to go home and change.

"I can understand why people buy up these condos so eagerly," Nicholas said standing in front of the living room windows. "If only there was a way to have such a view without doing so much environmental damage. To say nothing of the risk of living directly on the beach."

"It does beat Columbus on a five-above-zero day when you have nothing to look at but dirty snow," Melba said. "I suppose it's the ultimate dream for most retirees."

"And the ultimate nightmare for those who are trying to keep the status quo," Nicholas retorted. "They're invading from the north like Hannibal and bringing everything but the elephants. It's hard to keep up with essential services when you're inundated like that."

"Let's go," Ginny said, coming out of the bedroom. "The kids will be waiting for us."

Before they left, Melba took Mickey outside for a minute to do his duty.

"What a cute little dog," Nicholas said.

Ginny wondered if Nicholas always saw the best side of everything.

When they arrived at the beach, Beth saw her grandfather coming and jumped up from where a group of half a dozen children sat waiting.

"Grandpa, grandpa!" she shouted excitedly and hugged his waist. Ginny felt so guilty for having kept them apart.

Melba joined in with surprising zest. Since she never had children of her own, she'd always been a little stiff and formal around young people. But today she was totally relaxed and laughed and joked as if it were an every day occurrence to build sand castles on a Florida beach with half-a-dozen grade-schoolers. Was this transformation due to the sun, the beach, the Chardonnay, although surely that had worn off long ago? Or was it Nicholas' influence? He had a way of putting people at ease. Perhaps Melba was under his spell.

When they returned to the condo at 5:30, they were covered with patches of white sand that clung to the underside of their legs and arms. They washed off at the pool-side shower, shivering as the cold water drenched their overheated bodies. Both Melba and Ginny were tired from the long day, and Nicholas said that he must hurry home. He seemed to realize that their meeting had extended well beyond what Ginny had intended, and it was time for him to take his leave.

"It's been a wonderful day," he said. "I'm so glad I had the chance to meet you, Melba. I can see you two sisters have an exceptional relationship. You're to be envied."

Ginny put her arm around Melba's shoulder and hugged her. "We think we have something special."

"I'm glad you called me today because I'm leaving tomorrow for Michigan to visit my other daughter and her family for a couple of weeks. So I'll miss the next couple of lunches at Ramon's."

"It's been great," Melba said extending her hand.

Nicholas shook it warmly and left.

After he'd gone, they bathed and put on their nightclothes and bathrobes, deciding to spend a quiet evening at home watching television.

"Let's watch the news," Ginny said, "and then I'll fix a sandwich or something."

"No rush," Melba replied, already lying on the sofa. "I ate so much at lunch I'm not particularly hungry."

Ginny was reading the paper when she realized the weatherman was on and wondering whether it was going to stay fair for the rest of the week paid closer attention.

There was a note of caution in the weatherman's voice. "What was a small tropical depression is developing very rapidly into tropical storm Felipe in the southernmost part of the Gulf of Mexico, just west of the Yucatan Peninsula. It seems to be moving faster than usual, and at this point we're not sure what is going to develop, but we certainly need to keep our eye on it.

We advise all residents of the west coast to keep abreast of this one. It could turn into a hurricane."

"Oh, my," said Melba, sitting up. "Is this thing going to come toward us?"

"I don't know. This is my first hurricane season. But so far the one that came into the Gulf headed toward Texas. It'll probably go that way, too."

"My, God, I hope so."

"At least it isn't over by the Keys were Leland is," Ginny said.

TWENTY-SIX

They were seated at the drop leaf table in the living room watching the sun set. There were just enough clouds to reflect the orange and crimson rays, and they shimmered like Day-Glo paint in the western sky. Ginny had fixed tomato soup and grilled cheese sandwiches, but they were still so full from the seafood salad at the Summerhouse that they both picked at their meal.

"Absolutely sensational," mused Melba staring out the window.

"That's pretty close to a ten. Nine-and-a-half at least."

"God, but you're lucky."

"Am I? You haven't yet said what you think," Ginny said.

"About what?"

"About Nicholas, of course. I was hoping you'd bring it up, but I guess I'm going to have to."

"Honest, Ginny," Melba steepled her fingers together, "I was waiting for you to say something first."

Ginny shook her head in wonderment. "We haven't done this since we were kids, playing mind games with each other. Remember how we used to play coy about the boys we had crushes on? I thought we were over that forty years ago, yet here we are."

"Well, we haven't been in this kind of position in forty years either, you know. I feel pretty strange about this." Melba was looking uncomfortable. Ginny had never seen her sister when she didn't want to speak her mind.

"All I want to know is what you think of him."

"Being with him for one afternoon doesn't mean I really know him," Melba protested.

"But you must have some kind of impression. I'd just like to know what your gut reaction is."

Melba stared out the window at the sun which was now half way below the horizon. Ginny had noticed at that exact point it always seemed to hesitate as if the sea refused to accept it. It was some kind of illusion she was sure, but the infinitesimal pause always made her think of how her mother fought for one last breath as death overtook her many years ago. It was the way of the world, to resist finality.

"I'll be as honest as I can, Ginny. He seems like an intelligent, thoughtful, and very nice man. In fact, the word I would use to describe him is sweet."

"Sweet? That makes him sound like a wimp."

"Not really a wimp. Maybe too nice, though."

"How can anyone be too nice?" Ginny couldn't figure out what Melba was getting at.

"Remember how Mom always made pulled taffy for Christmas?"

"Sure. I loved the stuff."

"That's exactly what I mean. You loved it so much you would eat it until you'd be sick. Then you couldn't stand to look at it anymore. You have a habit of overdosing on sweets." Melba always seemed to bring up Ginny's childhood misadventures.

"And you think it would be the same with Nicholas."

"I don't know. But I think it's possible that someone who's so eternally congenial and pleasant might get to be pretty tiresome after a while."

"You're saying it's better to be around someone who blows his stack now and then like Leland does." Ginny couldn't believe this conversation. "Besides, you've only been with Nicholas for one day."

"I know, but I can tell pretty much that it's his basic temperament. And, well, it may sound crazy, but yes. I think it's good for the soul to air your grievances occasionally. Unrelieved politeness can be very stifling in a relationship."

"But Nicholas is so interested in everything I do. Leland couldn't care less about poetry or building sand castles."

"Let me ask you something, Ginny. You've been whining about that to me ever since you got to Florida. 'Leland won't do this and Leland won't do that.' But have you ever taken the slightest interest in his hobbies?"

"Golf and fishing? Good God, no."

"You've never tried them so I don't see how you can be so damn sure you wouldn't like them. It goes both ways, you know."

Ginny was disheartened. She always imagined that Melba was her staunchest ally, but it seemed she was mistaken. Melba didn't understand what she was going through, and it was obvious she didn't appreciate Nicholas' sensitivity and old-fashioned gallantry. She should have realized that Melba wouldn't sympathize with someone who was a poet; she was not an intellectual by any means, and Ginny was beginning to comprehend just how prosaic her sister's tastes really were.

She felt disappointed and let down. She wondered if she would ever feel exactly the same toward Melba again. This whole thing had been a mistake.

"You're saying I should forget Nicholas? Turn down his proposal?" Ginny asked.

"I'm not saying any such thing. I told you I wouldn't make any decisions for you. You asked for my initial reaction and you got it." She started to stack their dishes, putting one dirty plate on top of another which had always annoyed Ginny.

"But you think I'm not being fair to Leland."

"I'm saying that you've had thirty-eight years of a pretty darned good marriage. It's not been all perfect, but what marriage is? But you've been fighting him ever since he brought you down here. You have a closed mind on the subject and you won't even try to like it here."

"You're dead wrong, Melba. I've tried and tried. It's only tolerable when I'm with Nicholas."

"Okay, then. Do whatever it is you have to do."

Just then Mickey began to scratch at the front door.

"Oh, damn," said Melba, "that dog has lousy kidneys. I'll sneak him out, then help you clear up." She got the beach towel from the bedroom, covered him up and went out in the deepening dusk.

After she left, Ginny meant to get up and carry the stacked dishes to the dishwasher. But she couldn't move. She laid her head on her arms and cried softly, more confused, and unhappier now more than ever. But shortly she willed herself to get up, wipe her eyes, and go to the kitchen. She wasn't going to let Melba see she'd been crying.

When Ginny awoke the next morning the sky was overcast and the waves on the normally calm Gulf were high enough that the surfers were out, something of a rarity here.

She turned on the twenty-four-hour weather channel and learned that the tropical storm was rapidly reaching hurricane strength and was moving steadily up the center of the Gulf. Small craft warnings already had been posted up the entire west coast of the state and along the panhandle. The weatherman said it was too soon to predict where it might head, and it was particularly difficult to chart since it tended to wobble from side to side in its forward motion. He warned all coastal residents to stay informed.

Ginny was a little concerned about Leland although it seemed

192

that the storm was not headed due east toward the Keys. But he must be stranded in port somewhere with the advisories out. She suddenly realized that if the hurricane did come toward Sarasota, she and Melba were on their own. There was no way for Leland to get home.

"What's up?" Melba came out of her bedroom rubbing her eyes. Ginny repeated what she'd heard about the storm.

"What do we do if it comes this way?" Melba asked.

"Everybody's assigned to a shelter on the high ground. We're supposed to go to Phillipi Shores School on Tamiami Trail. The trick would be to get off the island. The traffic over the bridges will be backed up for miles they say. The thing to do is to go as soon as they have an alert."

"What about Mickey? Can I take Mickey with me?"

"No, they won't allow pets."

Melba's eyes grew wide. "You don't mean it. What am I supposed to do with him?"

"You'd have to leave him here. He'll be okay."

"No way, no way," Melba shook her head frantically. "Mickey's all I've got, and I wouldn't abandon him like that. You go. I'll stay here with Mickey."

"Come on now," Ginny said, trying to suppress her impatience. "Don't talk nonsense. Besides, I doubt very much it will come to that. The thing sure looks like it's headed for the Panhandle."

"Well, I mean what I say. I'm not leaving."

"Okay. Let's have breakfast." There was no sense in arguing over something that would probably never come to pass.

They decided to go to Myakka Park east of town although there was some threat of rain. Melba was anxious to give Mickey an outing, worrying about his being cooped up for so long. Anyway, it seemed senseless to mope around the condo waiting to see what the storm was going to do.

193

They packed a lunch to eat by the lake and drove the fifteen miles east on Route 72 to the park. The nucleus of the park was created from the one-time ranch of the Palmer family, who'd owned the *Chicago Tribune,* and represented a microcosm of early Florida, acres of live oak forest and palmetto scrub, and a small lake full of alligators. They boarded the small "train" of open cars pulled by a four-wheel-drive vehicle that toured the perimeter of the park where wild deer and armadillos and other indigenous creatures could be glimpsed in the thick vegetation. This was the Florida that had nearly disappeared, the turn-of-the-century Florida before runaway development had obscured so much of its natural beauty and mystery.

They had a pleasant day, although it would have been nicer if the sun had been shining and the wind not blowing so briskly. They talked about family and friends and neighbors in Columbus. They didn't discuss Nicholas or Leland.

By mid-afternoon when they were sitting on a bench at the side of the lake watching the array of egrets and herons and other waterfowl that called Myakka home, it began to sprinkle, the intermittent droplets launching intersecting circles on the surface of the water.

"Darn," Ginny said as a raindrop hit her squarely on the nose. "I didn't think it would start to rain this soon. I guess we might as well go home."

"It's been lovely here," Melba said gathering up her things. "I'm glad we came."

They ate a light supper on TV trays in front of the television, anxious to hear the latest weather conditions. The storm was west of Fort Myers now but still headed due north and gathering strength. A hurricane watch was in effect from Naples clear around to Biloxi. This one had to be monitored closely because it could go almost anywhere.

The phone rang and Ginny answered.

"What's the weather like there?" It was Leland.

"There was some light rain this afternoon. It's stopped though and it's just cloudy now."

"I don't like the looks of this one. We're stuck on Islamorada. If it looks at all like it's coming your way, get out of there fast. You don't want to be on the island if it hits."

"Melba says she won't leave Mickey."

"That's the most childish thing I've ever heard. Promise me that you'll get to a shelter."

"I will, I promise."

"I'll get home just as soon as we can get our boat back out again. You two take care of yourselves now."

"We will, Leland. You be careful, too."

"We're in no danger here. I'm just sorry as hell I left you at this time." His concern sounded real.

"How could you possibly know what was going to happen?"

"Just the same, I feel guilty about it. I feel like I've let you down."

"Come on, honey, it's not your fault. And we will be just fine," Ginny assured him.

"I'll be home as soon as I can. Love you."

"I love you, too." It came out automatically.

She hung up and looked toward Melba to see what her reaction was. Her face was expressionless.

"Leland says we must get out if the hurricane heads this way."

"You go on, then. I won't leave Mickey. He's all I've got."

"You're being ridiculous, Melba. No dog is that important." She was cross and she didn't mind showing it.

Melba started to cry. Ginny was alarmed. Her sister was the one who seemingly could deal with anything, the one everyone else always leaned on. And she was crying over a dog?

"What do you know?" Melba's voice rose with emotion. "You

have two men who care about you. All I ever had was Mack, and he's gone. You can say it's silly because you don't know any better." She began to cry harder. "God damn it, Ginny, it's not fair for you to have so much and me to have so little."

Ginny was dumbfounded. She'd never dreamed that Melba was jealous of her. Was that why she'd spoken scornfully of Nicholas; was it pure envy?

She saw it was useless to argue about leaving the island; Melba was fiercely determined to stay. The storm would probably pass them by anyway, so there was no sense in hassling over a moot point.

She went over to Melba who was still seated in the chair by the TV tray, her hand to her eyes trying to conceal her tears. Ginny picked up her free hand and held it in both of hers. She'd always thought of her sister as supremely capable of handling life's crises; it never occurred to her to feel sorry for her. Of course she sympathized when Mack died, but Melba seemed to make a remarkable adjustment, and Ginny greatly admired her ability to cope. Apparently much of it had been a charade.

"Melba, honey," she spoke hesitantly, "I never knew how you felt. It was thoughtless of me to ask you to come and meet Nicholas. I guess it looked like I was trying to rub it in, but that was the furthest thing from my mind."

Melba said nothing, but the tears continued to course down her cheeks.

Ginny continued. "I never knew how much you were hurting inside. I always expected you to comfort me when I was in trouble, but I thought you were so tough you could handle everything by yourself. I was wrong, wasn't I?"

"Just because I'm the oldest, everybody thinks I'm the strongest, too. Little do they know. But I guess it's my own fault because I never let down in front of any of you. But I'm damn tired of keeping it all to myself." She wiped her eyes and gave a brief self-deprecating smile. "The fact is, Ginny, I've always envied you."

This revelation shocked Ginny to her core.

Twenty-Seven

It was after two A.M. when the sirens and loudspeakers woke Ginny up. A pulsating blue light filtering between the cracks of the mini-blind gave an unworldly glow to the bedroom.

"Attention, attention," the sound echoed off the face of the high rise, "all residents are urged to evacuate the island now. The hurricane has abruptly turned east and is headed directly toward Sarasota. You must evacuate immediately."

There was a tapping at her door which opened before she could answer. Melba appeared in her nightgown, her hair sticking out at wild angles, her eyes heavy with sleep.

"I could hear a lot of commotion. What's going on?"

"The police are out there with bullhorns telling people to leave. The storm is coming right at us."

"Well, get dressed and get going then."

"No way, Melba, not without you."

"Any chance of getting into a motel with Mickey?"

"None. I just read in the paper they're all full with tourists. And everybody evacuating would be trying to get in if they weren't."

Ginny was tired of going over this with her sister but tried not to show it.

"Just how dangerous is it to stay here anyway?" Melba asked.

"The worst part is supposed to be the storm surge which can be fifteen or twenty feet high."

"But we're on the sixth floor. Surely it won't come up this far."

Ginny considered that. "That's true. The first floor on all new buildings has to be thirteen feet above mean high tide so we're way above that."

"So what's the worst it can do—go through the lobby? Your car might get wet, but it seems to me our chances are better here than trying to dodge hundreds of crazy drivers trying to get over that bridge. I'll bet your chances of a major fender bender are much greater than having a wave wash away your car." Now Melba seemed to be trying to excuse her intransigence.

Even under these circumstances, Ginny couldn't help but be amused. If Melba had been born twenty or thirty years later, she surely would have gone to law school. She could come up with logical-sounding arguments for anything she wanted or believed in.

"So you convinced me," she admitted. "Should we get up and see if we can find a local radio station?"

Melba made a pot of coffee while Ginny attempted to find an audible station that was broadcasting at this hour. The one she finally found confirmed what the police had been saying. Felipe, which was directly west of them in the center of the Gulf, had made an abrupt right-angle turn and was headed straight for Sarasota. It had changed direction so often before, no one could say with certainty that it would come ashore here, but for now it gave every appearance of maintaining a steady course. The announcer was urging all island residents, and those near the beach to evacuate to higher ground.

"I'd better find some candles and get out the kerosene lamp," Ginny said as they sat at the kitchen table sipping their coffee. "You realize that if the power goes off, we'll have to walk down to ground level to get out of here when it's over."

"Better down than up."

"You've got an answer for everything."

"Of course. I'm your big sister, aren't I?" Even though it was said facetiously, Ginny knew that Melba was giving notice that she was supposed to forget what had been said the night before. And that suited her just fine.

She had a dozen or so partially used candles in a kitchen drawer that she'd saved for such an occasion, and she found the kerosene lamp at the very back of a bottom cupboard. She dripped tallow into saucers and set the candles around the living room and kitchen. The kerosene lamp was left on the kitchen table.

"But how could you find them in the dark?" Melba asked.

"Good question. I ought to keep a flashlight with me, but it's in the glove compartment of the car. Do you think I should go down and get it?"

"Forget it," Melba said looking out the kitchen window. "You'd get run over if you did. The lot is swarming down there with people leaving."

Ginny walked over and peered out, too. People were streaming out of the building, and cars were jockeying for position, their headlights piercing the rain and darkness like a laser light show gone mad.

"Ah oh, what did I tell you?" Melba started to chuckle. "Someone just backed into someone else."

Now drivers began to honk as those who were held up by the accident showed their impatience. Soon the night was filled with the cacophony of braying horns as people demonstrated the level of tolerance they could sustain for their fellow man while under intense pressure.

"It looks like you were right, Melba." Ginny leaned closer to the window to get a better look. "That's going to be utter mayhem out there."

"Well, I'll tell you what I'm going to do," Melba said leaning back in her chair, "I'm too wide awake now to go back to bed so I'm going to curl up in the living room and try to finish the book I brought with me."

"You're sure the cool one."

"Cool, schmool. What do you want me to do, wring my hands and pace the floor? Let's be honest. I think everyone's over-reacting. I intend to relax and enjoy this. I look upon it as a new experience."

They both settled into living room chairs, Melba with her book, Ginny with a magazine. It was hard to believe there was a state of emergency; it was quiet except for the honking of horns as the procession to leave the island continued down Midnight Pass Road. Although Ginny felt some apprehension, she was glad not to be fighting the monstrous traffic jam. In spite of the tremendous growth on Siesta Key, Midnight Pass was the lone north-south road on the southern part of the island, and it was only three lanes wide including the turning lane. Even on a normal day, traffic was bumper-to-bumper. Anyone exiting the numerous condominium developments had to wait five or ten minutes to make a left turn. But attempts to widen Midnight Pass had always met with resistance from local residents who insisted it would encourage even more tourists to drive the length of the island.

Maybe Melba was right. This might be kind of fun. Here they were all snug in their home while the others were sitting in traffic gridlock, surely frustrated out of their minds, the cars overheating or running out of gas, the kids whining and crying in the back, and some jerk trying to sneak around everybody on the berm.

And, of course, in the end, the hurricane was bound to change directions again and all their misery would turn out to be unnecessary.

The phone rang, startling Ginny in her reverie. It must be Leland checking on them again. Ginny answered.

"It's Nicholas. I was checking to see if you two had left yet. Why are you still there?"

"We're not leaving."

"Are you crazy, Ginny?"

She was startled at his anger.

"We'll be okay. Melba won't leave without her dog. I thought you'd gone to Michigan."

"I got a late start. My john started to leak, and I had a minor flood in the bathroom, so I only got as far as Gainesville. They're evacuating people along the coast here so I've been listening to the radio. Do you realize you're liable to get a direct hit?"

"I'm sure we'll be all right up here on the sixth floor. Melba is simply adamant about not leaving Mickey alone here, and you know they won't allow dogs in the shelters."

"I can't believe you two. Let me talk to Melba, will you?"

"Okay. Hold on." She handed the phone to her sister. "Nicholas wants to talk to you."

"Nicholas? What on earth for? I thought he'd left town."

"He'll explain it to you."

Melba's expression was one of incredulity as she took the receiver. Ginny sat on the couch and stared out into the dark as the rain now ran in slick streams down the sliding glass doors, which ironically made her feel even more secure, as if she were enclosed in a cocoon, safe from the elements.

"Hello?" Melba said, "Nicholas? I thought you'd gone." She was silent as she listened.

"That's a shame. It never fails when you're trying to get away."

A long pause.

"No," she said testily. "Mickey is too precious to me. I absolutely will not go off and leave him alone here for God knows how long."

Another pause.

"Look, I'm sure this building was built to withstand any winds, and no storm surge is going to reach the sixth floor. We'll be perfectly okay."

Ginny could almost feel Melba's anger radiating from her. When she made up her mind about something, you might as well forget trying to talk her out of it. And she knew from past unhappy experiences that the more you tried, the more exasperated and entrenched Melba became.

"Here, you'd better talk to Ginny again. I'm not going to argue the point any more."

She handed the receiver back to her sister with a dramatic sweeping gesture and said, "You deal with him. I can't."

"Yes?" She said cautiously because she didn't know what to expect.

"Look," Nicholas' voice had a pleading quality, "I'm really worried about you two, and I think you should get out immediately."

"I can see Midnight Pass from my kitchen window and the cars are scarcely moving out there. If the storm does hit here we would probably be in the middle of Stickney Point Bridge. I think we're safer where we are."

"Okay, okay. I can see I'm not going to change your mind. Will you do this then? Fill up your tubs and washing machine with water in case the water supply is cut off and you can't get out. And draw your drapes so if any windows break, you won't get hit by flying glass. Will you do that much?"

"Aren't you being a bit dramatic?"

"Oh, Ginny, you are so naive."

"Thanks a lot." No wonder Melba was irritated with him. He wouldn't quit.

"Humor me, will you please?"

"If I must. Are you going on to Michigan?" she asked to change the subject.

"No, I'll stay here till the all clear, and then I'm coming back to Sarasota. I want to make sure my house is okay."

"Too bad you're not home. We'd come stay with you."

"If I thought I could make it back before the storm, I'd do it just to get you off the island. But there's no way. And I don't have a key hidden under the mat or anything."

"Well, give us a call when you get back so we can reassure you we made it through the storm," Ginny said.

"I'll come out there if they'll let me."

"Okay. Thanks for caring. Goodbye, Nicholas." She hung up the phone gently, touched by his concern although still annoyed by his attitude that they didn't have good sense.

When she went back to the living room, Melba was sitting on the couch, hugging her knees the way she often did when she was out of sorts.

"Well, did you give in?" she glared at Ginny.

"You know I'm not going to leave. I did promise him I'd fill the tub and washing machine with water so we'll be sure to have some if the supply gets cut off."

"I take back my comment that he's nothing but sweetness and light. He was so persistent I wanted to knock his block off."

Ginny couldn't help but laugh. "Honestly, Melba, you have a lot of guts complaining about someone else's stubbornness. It's your obstinacy that got him so mad in the first place."

Melba didn't answer but grinned sheepishly, picked up her book, and settled back onto the davenport.

Ginny went to the bathroom, scoured the tub, and filled it to the top. The next thing she knew Mickey was beside her, his front paws on the side of the tub, lapping at the water. She put her arm around the scruffy old dog's neck and hugged him. "You idiot dog. You get us into more damn trouble. Now for

God's sake don't contaminate our drinking water." She led him from the bathroom and closed the door.

She opened the bi-fold door in the hallway that hid the washer and dryer and filled the washing machine to capacity. Mickey stood beside her, ears alert, as if waiting for something momentous to happen.

"Come on in the living room," she said patting his head. "You can keep us company while we wait this thing out."

Before sitting down again, she pulled all the drapes closed. The rain which earlier had made her feel cozy and safe was coming down harder now, pelting the balcony with the rumbling sound of a small waterfall, and the wind was beginning to make eerie noises as it blew around the corners of the building. Mickey, who in his old age slept through almost anything, nuzzled Melba's hand, whining and prancing nervously, as if some unseen tormentor was nipping at his feet.

"What's the matter, Mickey?" Melba asked, petting him and trying to calm him down. "Does the wind scare you?" She put her hands behind his ears and massaged his neck. "Poor baby," she crooned, "Mama is going to take care of you."

They scarcely talked during the next hour, each wrapped in her own thoughts. Melba seemed perfectly relaxed, and Ginny couldn't tell whether she was faking it or not. Mickey's nervousness was rubbing off on her though. She wanted something to happen, an all-clear signal, the storm to come on through, anything to break the tension of waiting . . .

Twenty-Eight

It should have been dawn, but the eastern sky was as dark as midnight as the storm increased in intensity. The wind howled like banshees as it was deflected around the sides of the building, and the rain had gone from staccato to a steady roar against the windows. Mickey now sat trembling and spooked under a lamp table, whining like a child who had gone past hysteria into an exhausted whimper, and Melba seemed unable to calm him.

Ginny tried bravely to ignore it all and continued reading, but with an ominous click, like the sound of a gigantic pistol being cocked, the lights went out, throwing the room into total darkness.

"Oh, God," she wailed. "Here we go!"

"Where are the matches?" Melba demanded. "You act like you've never had a power outage before."

Ginny could feel the color rising in her cheeks and was thankful Melba couldn't see her. She reached into her robe pocket and pulled out a matchbook, felt around the table beside her until she touched the candlestick and lit it.

She then lit the rest of the candles around the room and brought in the kerosene lamp from the kitchen.

"Now, isn't this cozy?" Melba asked, gesturing at the flickering lights that caused eerie shadows to sway and bow on the walls as if genuflecting to the gods. Somehow Ginny wasn't reassured. The pandemonium of the storm seemed to be steadily increasing.

Ginny started to respond with as upbeat an answer as she could muster, but before she could utter the first words the window exploded with a tumultuous roar. The drapes stood straight out from the rod as if levitated by invisible strings, and a maelstrom of rain mixed with shards of glass was hurled by the force of the wind into every corner of the room. Ginny screamed and covered her face with her hands, and Melba flattened herself on the sofa, trying to protect her head with her book. All the candles were blown out, and only the kerosene lamp miraculously sent a feeble wavering light over the scene of destruction.

It was a few seconds before Ginny recovered enough to be certain of what had happened. But one thing she knew for sure: their cozy little myth of being safe and sound had vanished in that instant. She could feel rivulets running down her face and wiped her hand across her forehead, nearly fainting when she saw her palm covered with watery blood. She stumbled over to the mirror that hung on the wall opposite what used to be the window and checked her image in the dim light. She had a one-inch gash at her scalp line and a minor prick on her left cheek, but nothing too serious.

She hurried back to Melba who was sitting dazedly on the couch, picking pieces of window off the cushions. There was a tear and a little blood on her left sleeve, but otherwise she seemed all right.

The wind and rain were destroying the living room. Most of the glass lay in jagged pieces on the table in front of the window and on the carpet. The cushions on the couch and chair were turning into a soggy mess, and the white rug looked like the matted fur of a dog who'd been swimming. The whole scene was bizarre, and surreal.

"Let's get in the hall bathroom," Ginny yelled at Melba. "There are no windows there and it should be safer."

Melba stared at her but did not respond.

Ginny picked up the kerosene lamp and went over to help her sister off the couch.

"Where's Mickey?" It was as if Melba had suddenly awakened from a dream. Her eyes were wild and her voice shrill and anxious. Ginny had forgotten the dog in the pandemonium. She looked under the table where he'd been huddled in pure terror just a few minutes earlier, but he was gone. Instead there was a dark stain where he'd been sitting, and leading from it was a pinkish trail that disappeared down the hallway. Leaving Melba sitting there in a near catatonic state, Ginny followed the trail which grew ominously darker the further she went. It led to her bedroom on the front side of the condo, much to her relief, because she didn't want to be near any windows on the Gulf side. Mickey lay near the bed, a fragment of glass, surprising small and nonlethal-looking, protruding from his neck. His fur was matted with blood in a large red circle that extended over the left side of his head and down over half his belly and back. She knelt beside him and could see he was panting slowly, laboriously, and she knew he'd lost too much blood to survive. She was afraid that if she attempted to remove the glass shard it would only hasten his death. There didn't seem to be much she could do.

She saw something move out of the corner of her eye and turned to see Melba, soaked and disheveled, standing in the doorway and holding onto the door frame as if she might collapse if she let go. Ginny stood up and walked over to her, putting her arms around her sister, feeling the trembling of her body whether from fear, grief, or cold she didn't know. She searched for comforting words, but even if she knew what to say, the din of the storm had become too loud for her to be heard anyway. All she could do was weep.

But Melba pushed her away and stumbled toward Mickey,

whose form was bathed in the soft light of the kerosene lamp Ginny had set on the floor nearby. Sitting on the floor beside him, she raised his head and cradled it in her lap, completely unmindful that she was staining her pink housecoat with his blood. She rocked back and forth, apparently crooning to him as she would to a sick child, but the sounds were lost in the storm's clamor.

Ginny knew it was risky to stay in any room with windows. "Let's get into the bath where it's safer," she yelled, touching Melba's arm to get her attention. But she realized that Melba could not hear what she was saying. "Bath," Ginny screamed, exaggerating her lip movements, hoping she could read her lips. "Bath," she screamed again, pointing toward the hall.

Melba shook her head no and continued to rock the lifeless dog. Ginny had known her sister to be stubborn and willful, but never before had she acted with such complete disregard for common sense. It was like being with a total stranger. This was not the practical and prudent Melba who was as much a mother figure as sibling. This disintegration of her sister's personality was more frightening than the frenzy of the storm.

She went around in front of Melba, knelt down and put her hands on her shoulders, commanding her attention, praying the shock method would work. "He's dead," she screamed above the din, "Mickey's dead."

Melba looked at her with such disbelief and grief that Ginny instantly regretted saying it. It was a moment of déjà vu; she'd seen that same look on her face at Mack's funeral. She'd heard of people who took the death of a pet as hard as that of a loved one, but she'd never been able to understand such an attachment to an animal.

Even though Ginny's words apparently had gotten through, Melba made no move to leave the room. She continued to rock the dog's body and croon to it. Ginny realized then that nothing she said or did would cause her sister to move, and she wasn't going to leave her alone. She got up, took a pillow from the bed, propped it vertically against the bottom of the bed and sat down against it. A few minutes later she got up again, took the quilted spread and hung it over the curtain rod. If that window was going to blow in, maybe the spread would catch most of the glass.

It seemed to her that the building was vibrating now. She could actually feel a shuddering sensation in the floor. Until twenty minutes ago she'd thought of this as an adventure, something she could share in vivid detail with Leland and Donald and Susan (and Nicholas of course). It was the kind of experience one could enlarge upon in each retelling, one of those favorite tales that becomes an integral part of family history, improving with age like a good wine.

But now the situation had become very ugly and frightening and she was scared as hell. She was petrified and no one was there to comfort or reassure her. When she hurt her knee, she felt the same sort of terror as she fell. She'd watched the ground coming up at her and wondered if she was going to die or be paralyzed or horribly injured. But at least that terror was short-lived. Now she fervently wished she could faint or go to sleep or fall into some state of limbo as Melba seemed to have done. Anything was better than sitting there gripped in a paralyzing fear that caused her hands to shake visibly, her stomach to be wracked by an endless spasm, and that sent iciness through her veins that belied the fact the room had become hot and clammy without air conditioning.

It was forty-five minutes later when the noise miraculously subsided. Neither of them had moved, although Melba had become quiet. But she still held Mickey and much of the front of her robe was stained with his blood. Suddenly, sunshine penetrated the room around the edges of the spread that shielded the window.

Ginny jumped up and yanked off the spread, pulling the blinds up to peer out. The eastern sky was still black, but directly above them was a patch of blue through which the sun shone brightly. She felt such a surge of joy and relief she could have danced about the room until she remembered that it must the eye of the storm which meant they were only halfway through it.

The view of the parking lot did nothing to reassure her. She'd seen such devastation only on television; to be witnessing the real thing was infinitely more terrifying. Water covered everything and it appeared to be several feet deep. Trees had been stripped of their leaves and blossoms, and many had been broken off, leaving ragged stumps. It reminded her of years ago when they began to fill a reservoir north of Columbus, and the once beautiful valley became a pond full of tree skeletons. Downed lines sputtered like giant sparklers as they bobbed and dragged in the flooded road.

The few cars that had been left in the parking lot had been pushed by waves or blown into poles or what was left of the wooden privacy fence that marked the border of the property. Her car had been shoved against a light post with a Volkswagen bug half lifted onto her fender. Debris was everywhere, boards and signs and beach furniture floating on the water.

She knew she must go check out the living room, although her legs felt as if they had hundred pound weights tied to them. Melba seemed unaware of the change; she sat motionless, unresponsive. Ginny stepped around her and walked slowly, reluctantly down the hall.

The scene was worse than she'd imagined. The drapes hung limply now that the wind had stopped, half pulled off the rod and laying in sodden heaps on the floor. Everything in the room was drenched and covered with pieces of glass. The upholstered pieces were stained and dark from the soaked padding. She wasn't particularly upset about the yellow davenport and chair that had seemed inhospitable anyway, but she was heartbroken over her favorite chair, the swivel rocker. The floral print had large murky splotches she knew would never fade. The cherry table by the window that had been her grandmother's had turned white from the soaking, and her majolica plates and figurines were lying like bits of colorful confetti on the soggy carpet where they'd been swept by the force of the wind.

She stepped closer to the window, although reluctant to get too near. The empty space where there had been glass made her feel too vulnerable. What she saw made her back up a step in horror.

Instead of a wide beach guarded by dunes and a swimming pool and terrace behind the condominium, there was now only water, angry waves lapping up to and apparently even through the building. Pieces of lounge chairs and umbrella-topped tables bobbed in the surf along with other debris. No wonder the floor vibrated. Would the building hold up under more of this assault? To outward appearances their building seemed to be reasonably well built; there were no obvious flaws. But how were they to know whether the foundation was structurally sound or not?

The sun was still shining on Siesta Key, but not far to the west the clouds were blacker than ever, and it wouldn't be long until the whole terrifying assault began all over again. And there wasn't one damn thing she could do to be any safer. The sixth floor should be above any tidal surge. But would the force of it topple the building? *Oh, God, she was so scared.*

Twenty-Nine

"Ginny?"

She turned to see Melba standing at the far edge of the living room. She looked so helpless and frightened, like a small child who'd just awakened from a nightmare. "We're going to die, aren't we?"

"Of course not." Did she actually say those words? Ginny couldn't believe she could sound so calm and assured when she was so terrified. But she couldn't let Melba see her fear, not when she was so devastated by Mickey's death. That was the whole thing. She understood it now. Melba unconsciously had endowed her dog with the power to keep her safe, to protect her, even though in reality he was probably one of the most cowardly dogs Ginny had ever seen. But Melba needed to project the feeling of security that Mack had given her onto someone or something else. And Mickey was that something. Now that her "protector" was gone, her self confidence had disintegrated.

Ginny walked over to her sister and took her hand. She needed to talk to her, make her understand before the wind started up again and they could no longer hear each other.

"We'll be okay," she said. "This is the eye of the storm but the winds will begin again soon. We'll be much safer if we stay in the bathroom." She wished she felt half as confident as she sounded. "We need to stay away from the windows."

Melba nodded in agreement and stood dejectedly, waiting for

Ginny to lead her there. She took Melba's elbow and guided her into the bath and sat her on the toilet seat lid before going to the bedroom. Mickey's body had been laid upon the bed, the bedspread covering him like a shroud.

She stuck a pillow under each arm and picked up the kerosene lamp thinking how precious light became when it wasn't available at the flick of a light switch. She joined Melba in the bathroom. Her sister was weeping softly now, which reassured Ginny. She would rather have her showing signs of normal grief than behaving like a zombie. She tucked one pillow behind Melba's back and sat down on the floor, placing the other pillow against the edge of the tub and leaning back against it. How thankful she was that she at least had heeded Nicholas' plea to fill the tub with water. It might be a long while before they could get out of there, if they survived at all.

Soon the wind picked up again and the cacophony was greater than ever. She'd read somewhere that the second half of the storm could be worse than the first—something about the winds going in the opposite direction. She was very thankful to be away from any windows. And it wasn't long before she thought she heard the sound of breaking glass, although it was very nearly impossible to distinguish sounds in the clamor. She hugged her knees tightly, trying to prevent the tremors that coursed through her body like electric shocks. She felt humiliated and humbled to realize she was such a coward, but tried to reassure herself with the thought that any reasonably intelligent person had every right to be terrified in such a predicament. Only the foolish and ignorant could claim they had no fear.

She could feel vibrations again only worse than before. Closing her eyes and praying as fervently as she knew how, she asked God to spare them. She couldn't think of any promises to make in exchange for her life, like offering to be a missionary in Africa, solely to bribe God. She lived her life as best she knew how, making mistakes like everyone else but never deliberately doing anything hurtful or cruel. She didn't know whether it was fair to ask God to single them out to be spared when people were dying every day in shocking and terrible ways. But it never hurt to try.

A sudden jolt shook the walls, and Ginny thought her heart had stopped for good. She knew that the storm surge must have hit the building, and she waited for the floor to tilt, the ceiling to fall in. She held her breath, expecting at any second to be thrown or dropped into the roaring surf . . . but nothing happened.

She felt a touch and opened her eyes to see Melba, her face white even in the soft light of the kerosene lamp, groping for her hand. She took her sister's clammy hand in her own, and they sat there for the next hour, unmoving, unable to speak above the roar, each dealing with her own fears and questions and regrets. But the touch of Melba's hand brought her comfort. She didn't think she could have dealt with this alone; even though Melba had been uncharacteristically helpless, having her there made all the difference in the world.

After what seemed like an eternity, but according to her watch had been an hour and twenty-five minutes, the din seemed to be lessening. Could it be the storm was winding down, and their building still stood? The roar gradually lessened until at last it sounded like a normal rainstorm.

She pressed Melba's hand. "I think we've made it," she said, the first words she'd uttered since the eye of the storm passed through. "Let's go check things out."

She went out into the living room. Whatever had not been smashed before, which was little, now lay in pieces on the soaked carpet. Her pictures had been blown off the walls, the glass smashed and the watercolors washed away. The curtains had been torn completely off the rods and blown against the far wall. Everything was in total ruins. But, oddly, Ginny felt very little anguish over her furnishings that had been destroyed. She was still on such a high from being spared that it really didn't seem to matter that much. Material things were just things after all.

Standing back from the space that was once the picture window, she stood on tiptoe and peered out. The water seemed higher now, but it was impossible to judge just how high from six floors up. Even more debris floated on the choppy water which was being dashed again and again against the building, only to be pulled back to begin the process all over again like some frenzied ritual.

Melba was at her side now. "How high do you suppose that is?" Her voice sounded firm, as if she'd regained some of her old assuredness.

"It's probably well up in the lobby anyway. In fact, some of that stuff that's floating looks like lobby furniture. See that big brown thing?"

Melba craned her neck. "What is it?"

"I think that's the new electric organ that the women's group just bought with their bazaar money. It seems to be upside down so it's hard to tell."

"So what do we do now?" Melba, even though she seemed much more like her old self, apparently was going to continue to defer to Ginny to make decisions.

"Well, the first thing, I think, is to get dressed."

Melba looked down at her bloodied housecoat and appeared shocked by it, as if she'd been unaware that Mickey had bled on it. "Oh, yes," she said, "I'll have to throw this away, won't I?"

"And then," Ginny continued, wondering how to say it to Melba without sending her spiraling into another state of shock, "we need to do something about Mickey. It's hot in here without the air conditioning." She hoped Melba would understand what she meant without having to spell it out.

She nodded her head vaguely without saying anything.

Ginny was reluctant to go into her bedroom where Mickey's body lay on the bed, but all of her clothes were in there. Melba followed her down the hall and went into the guest room.

"The window's gone in here," she called out. Ginny crossed the hall to find that room in shambles, too. The bed, night stands and dresser were all soaked and the lamps had been broken.

"I thought I heard it breaking while we were in the bathroom," she said.

Melba opened the closet door and looked inside. "Things look pretty dry in here," she said. "There are a few wet spots and some water on the floor where it must have blown in under the door, but it doesn't look too bad."

"What about the clothes in the drawers?" Ginny asked.

Melba pulled out the top drawer to reveal sopping underwear. "Good Lord," she said, "I can't believe the rain could get inside the drawers."

"The wind was probably blowing more than a hundred miles an hour. That will get the rain into some pretty strange places."

"Well, I can't wear wet underwear."

"I'd loan you mine, but it might be a bit snug."

"Snug?" Melba actually laughed. "Babe, you couldn't pry me into it with a shoehorn. But thanks for suggesting it anyway."

Ginny was enormously relieved to hear Melba's attempt at humor. "I guess you'll have bobbing boobs, but then who's around to see? Let's hang some of this over the shower rod to dry out."

Ginny's bedroom windows were still intact so her clothes were dry. She dressed in slacks and a short-sleeved blouse, mulling over in her mind how they were going to dispose of Mickey's body. She knew it would begin to decompose soon in the heat, but until the water subsided, they wouldn't be able to get out of the building. And God knew how long it would be before the authorities could get to the Key. She wondered if the bridges were still intact. The storm had been so ferocious that anything could have happened.

"Now what?" Melba was standing in the bedroom door. She was wearing a loose-fitting sweater and slacks, and Ginny was shocked to realize how old her sister looked without the help of undergarments. Her sagging breasts and lumpy hips added years to her age. It was the first time she'd ever thought of Melba as being on the verge of "old." And she was only nine years older than Ginny herself.

"I'm going to walk down the outside stairs to see exactly how high the water is. I can't tell from up here."

"Well, I'm going with you then."

The women stepped out onto the sixth floor balcony in a light rain. In spite of the destruction inside, they were still unprepared for the scene outside. The parking lot was now a debris-filled lake with trees, signs, pieces of roofs, furniture, and all kinds of unidentifiable objects floating on the still choppy waters. Only the tops of the several cars left there could be seen, and they'd been pushed around and tipped as if playthings.

Across Midnight Pass Road where there'd been a couple of older private homes sandwiched between high rise condominiums, there were now only piles of debris, with timbers floating among pieces of roof and door frames sticking up like war-ravaged remains in the flooded lots. Ginny could see what appeared to be the top of a refrigerator floating inside the broken walls, and a tricycle, one of those large three-wheeled kind that senior citizens favored, hanging like the skeleton of some dead thing in the broken branches of a pepper tree. She was more surprised and thankful than ever that Tranquility Gardens had resisted the force of the water that had destroyed so much.

Gingerly she made her way down the stairwell with Melba

following her. She wondered why it was intact when so much else had been torn apart but guessed that the building had protected it. If the stairs had been on the Gulf side, she was sure they would have been destroyed, and she and Melba would be trapped on the sixth floor.

By the time they reached the third floor balcony they could tell how high the storm surge had been. Everything was intact as far as the landing halfway between the second and third floors, but below that the stairs were badly damaged with treads missing, and the railing was dangling where it had been pulled loose on one end. Seaweed and other debris clung to the remaining steps like green blemishes.

The women gingerly walked down to the landing, but it seemed too dangerous to proceed any further.

"Look," Melba pointed toward the closest second floor window. The glass was broken out and wet and tattered curtains sagged half in and half out of the window. It was hard to make out the interior but it looked as though a table was upended just inside. It would have been the kitchen eating area.

"The storm surge must have come up to here," Ginny said. "It looks like most of the windows on this floor were broken. The wave just went right through the building."

"I can't believe the building stood up under it. I was sure we were going to die." Melba's voice broke as she spoke.

"I guess God had other plans for us. And remember, it isn't going to be any picnic till we can get out of here."

The remaining water was about halfway up the ground floor windows, or rather where the windows had been. Gaping holes were all that were left of the picture windows of the first floor which had served as office, lobby, and meeting room. Debris like folding chairs, the coffee pot from the kitchenette area of the meeting room, and soggy remnants from the small library floated in and out of the building with the waves as if torn between remaining in their rightful spot in the building or escaping to the freedom of the sea.

"Looks like we're not going anywhere for a while." Ginny knew she was belaboring the obvious, but she wasn't eager to bring up the next subject they had to discuss which was what to do with Mickey.

"Let's go back up before we're soaked," Melba said, although the rain was no more than a fine mist now. As they silently climbed the stairs back to their floor, Ginny tried to come up with an idea of how to dispose of the dog, but in their situation there didn't seem to be any solution.

When they got back to the condo, Melba asked, "Do you have a turkey roaster and some rope?"

"What on earth do you want with those?"

"I think Mickey would fit in the roasting pan. We could tie the lid on, carry it down the stairs as far as we could go, and then lower it with rope into the water."

"And . . . ?"

"And then we'll just let him float away. That's sort of like scattering ashes over the water only we can't cremate him. Do you have a better idea?"

"No."

"We have to do something . . ."

Ginny nodded solemnly. She was amazed that Melba was so calm after the way she'd come apart during the storm. But she'd always admired her sister's resilience, and apparently Melba was bounding back once again. "Okay, that's what we'll do then."

They went into the kitchen, which had escaped much of the destruction since it faced away from the Gulf, and Ginny found the large turkey roaster in the bottom cupboard.

"Before we get Mickey, there's something I want to do," she said. She went to the linen closet and brought back a pale pink satin sheet. "I bought this in a moment of extreme weakness," she said. "I had trouble sleeping at night even with the air conditioning, and I thought it might be cooler to sleep on satin."

Her sister nodded.

"Besides," she smiled and could feel the warmth of a blush in her cheeks, "I thought it might be kind of sexy."

"Well, was it?" Melba's face didn't show a trace of flippancy.

"I never found out. Leland couldn't stand the thought of sleeping on satin so we never used them."

Melba's lips twitched in an effort not to grin. "That's too bad."

Back to reality thought Ginny. "I want to line the roaster with this, make it seem more like a real casket."

Melba's face softened. "That's real sweet, Ginny. I appreciate it." She placed the folded sheet in the roaster, smoothing it so that it lined the bottom and sides, and carried it and the lid back to the bedroom. Before following her, Ginny got a ball of heavy twine from a kitchen drawer along with a knife.

Together the women lifted the now stiff body of Mickey and laid him in the roaster. With his legs tucked under him, he barely fit. They placed the lid over him and tied the handles at each end together with twine.

Melba picked up the roaster, the strain showing in her face.

"Here, let me help you," Ginny said, "it looks heavy."

"I can manage. I really want to do this." Melba headed for the door, Ginny following behind.

They retraced their steps down to the landing between the second and third floors, and Melba set down her burden, straightening up slowly and massaging her shoulders. "He's heavier than I thought, carrying him like this. Do you think it will float?"

"If all that furniture can float, surely this can."

Ginny cut two long pieces of twine and tied a long loop to

each handle.

"Now we'll just lower it slowly till it touches the water," she said handing one piece to Melba.

"Give me a minute, please." Melba knelt beside the makeshift coffin and put her hands on top. "Mickey, you were a great comfort to me, and I'm going to miss you terribly. I know you didn't have much time left anyway as old as you were, but that was a pretty terrible way to die. I guess I'm to blame for it and I'll never forgive myself. Rest in peace, my baby." When she stood up, her tears were flowing freely.

Ginny was so touched and saddened that she hugged her sister fiercely. She'd been wrong to belittle Melba's attachment to Mickey, even if she'd never voiced her disparagement.

"You can't blame yourself, Melba. You risked your own life because you wouldn't leave him alone. It was just a freak thing."

Melba simply shook her head. "Let's get it over with."

They each took a handle and picked up the roaster and balanced it on the railing. Slowly they lowered it over the side, letting out the twine inch by inch till at last it reached the water. It settled into the choppy waves as if it had always belonged to the sea. They dropped the twine and watched as it bobbed gracefully on the surface moving forward and then back with the waves but inching its way slowly eastward toward the road. Ginny hoped it would somehow find its way to the Gulf and be carried out into the vast emptiness of the sea rather than ending up caught up in some debris on the island. But she had no control over that. All she could do was pray that somehow it would move in the right direction eventually avoiding all the traps that waited to prevent it from reaching the freedom of open spaces.

Thirty

Back in the condo they rummaged through the cupboards for something to eat. The electricity had been off for hours now, and they knew that the food in the refrigerator wouldn't keep long, so they decided to eat that first.

"Believe it or not I'm starved," Melba said. "Somehow it doesn't seem appropriate to think of food at a time like this, but what's it been—about twenty-four hours since we've eaten?"

"Not since dinner last night," Ginny said piling up cheese and cold cuts on wheat bread. "You can't be any hungrier than I am."

They both ate heartily, deciding to split the remains of a box of already melting ice cream between them.

"I feel like a pig," Melba said, eyeing a heaping bowl of vanilla-chocolate swirl that was on the verge of being soup.

"Well, don't feel guilty. We'd just have to throw it out if we didn't eat it right away."

They were afraid to use what water might be in the taps so they brought a bowlful from the tub into the kitchen to rinse off their dishes. It wasn't till they'd stacked them in the drainer that it occurred to Ginny how ludicrous it was to be washing dishes in face of the fact that the rest of the condo lay in ruins.

"Now what?" Melba asked as they finished.

"I don't know. I feel like we ought to do something to clean up the living room, but the furniture is soaked and we can't sit in there. Same way with your bedroom. To tell you the truth I feel completely washed out. Since my bedroom's the only place intact, why don't we just go to bed in there?"

Melba agreed that she was exhausted, too. Both of them averted their eyes as they passed through the corner of the living room on their way to the bedroom. It was too painful to look at the destruction.

A bloodstain marred the bedspread where Mickey had lain.

"I'm sorry," Melba said, gathering it up in her arms, "I'm afraid it's ruined."

"It doesn't matter." Ginny took it from her and stuffed it in her hamper. When Melba wasn't around she would dispose of it.

Ginny loaned her sister a nightgown, one that was very loose fitting that she could wear, and they climbed into bed.

"Do you realize we haven't slept in the same bed together since I was twelve and you were three?" Melba could always remember in detail even the most trivial events of their childhood.

"Just so you don't snore," Ginny said.

"I don't think so, but no one's been around to tell me lately," Melba said without a trace of self pity.

Even though it had not yet gotten dark, the women soon dozed off, their bodies so exhausted from the hours of extreme tension that the bed would shake as tight muscles caused legs to jump and twitch, startling Ginny briefly from her sleep. Once in the night she awoke to find that Melba had thrown her arm across her in a dreamy embrace. Perhaps in her sleep she thought she was hugging Mack, but Ginny felt secure in their closeness.

It was just after daybreak that the noise awoke Ginny. It was like a rerun of two days earlier when the loudspeakers in the night had warned them of the approaching storm. For a split second she thought it was the same night, that she had dozed off momentarily, but then the memory of all that had happened swept over her with such painful intensity it was like a physical blow. She got out of bed and peered out the window and saw a motor boat moving slowly down Midnight Pass Road, or rather where the road used to be. Two men in slickers were seated and one was standing, speaking into a bullhorn.

"Is there anyone marooned out there?" The voice came echoing across the water that still covered the landscape. "We've come to get you out."

"We're up here!" Ginny shouted as loud as she could, waving her hand so they would see her.

"Huh, what?" Melba sat up drowsily. "What's going on?"

"Over here!" Ginny shouted again as the men began to turn the boat toward their building. She turned to her sister. "It looks like we're getting rescued. We'd better get some clothes on."

"God, yes." Melba was sitting up fully awake now. "Nobody's going to see me like this."

Melba's underwear had dried in the bathroom, and she put on the slacks and sweater she'd worn the day before. Ginny dressed hurriedly, too.

They were out the door on the sixth floor balcony by the time the boat pulled up in front of the high rise. The men had thrown a rope around the remains of the stairs to steady it just above the first floor level where the water still flowed in and out of the building. The exterior elevators were obviously not working so they'd have to go back down the stairs to reach the boat.

"We'll take you ladies over to the shelter on the mainland," yelled the man who'd been using the bullhorn. "Are you all right?"

"We're fine," Ginny called over the railing of the balcony. She and Melba got their purses, the only possession they could take with them, and walked down the stairs as far as they could go.

From there they had an eight-foot drop to the boat.

The man who had spoken, looking authoritative and strong, his rugged face picture-perfect for the role of rescuer-hero, stood in the middle of the boat as the other men held it steady against the remains of the stairs. "If you ladies will sit on that last step and then push yourself off, I'll catch you."

"Are you sure about that?" Ginny was dubious. "I just busted up my knee last year. I'm not anxious to hurt it again."

"I'm not going to let you get hurt. Trust me."

"I'll go first," Melba said, sitting down on the step, "to show you it's okay." She sat there a moment as if to summon up her courage, and then leaned forward and rather gracefully jumped into his arms. The boat bounded precariously for a few seconds, but as soon as Melba sat down, the men were able to stop its rocking.

"Next." The man held open his arms to Ginny. She didn't want to do this. She still occasionally had nightmares about falling off the ladder, and the fear of re-injuring her knee was constantly with her. But she couldn't sit there forever. These men had other people to rescue. She closed her eyes, a silly impulse she knew, and pushed herself off the step. She felt strong arms encircle her waist, a frightening rocking motion as the boat reacted to her weight, and she opened her eyes to see the man's smiling face.

"See? You made it just fine."

He helped her to the seat beside Melba who put her arm around her waist. "You okay?" she asked.

She nodded mutely. It was as if, in jumping into the boat, she had jumped into the real world out of a dream, or a nightmare.

She had functioned well during the past two days, perhaps even better than she could have hoped to perform under such circumstances. But it was all in sort of a haze, almost with a feeling of being totally unrelated to her body. She'd done all the things she was supposed to do but in a detached way. She couldn't explain it; she simply had been on automatic pilot.

But now she didn't have to be in charge any more. These men were going to take care of her and see that she got to the shelter where she should have been all along. She could let down her defenses now. In spite of the heat, she began to shake as if chilled.

She felt like a fool but she couldn't stop shaking, and she knew everyone was aware of it. Then Melba, her arm still around her waist, squeezed her tightly and whispered, "You were absolutely terrific, you know it?"

This unlocked the tears, and Ginny wept as they proceeded down the road, the man in front of them calling to survivors on his bullhorn.

About half a block further on, they came upon a wet and bedraggled man sitting on the roof of a car in the middle of a condominium parking lot. He waved to them with such obvious exhaustion, Ginny was afraid he would collapse and fall off into the water before they could reach him. He was not a young man, and whatever had happened during the storm had taken an enormous toll.

The men guided the boat carefully beside him. As they reached over to help him off the car, he literally fell into their arms crying, "You've got to help my wife."

"Where is she?" asked the man with the bullhorn.

"She's in our apartment," he said pointing toward the nearest building. "I think she's had a heart attack. She collapsed a couple of hours ago. I knew I had to get help, and I thought I could wade through the water and find someone to help me. But the current was so strong, I couldn't walk against it, and it almost carried me away. I grabbed at this car and climbed up on top. Otherwise I'd be floating out in the bay."

"What number is your apartment?" the man who was guiding the boat asked as he slowly directed them toward the front entrance of the building. The stairs in this high rise were on the inside so they would have to wade into the lobby to get upstairs. Luckily it was on higher ground on the east side of the road so the water wasn't as deep as it had been at Tranquility Gardens.

"Three eighteen." The distraught man tried to climb out of the boat to accompany the two rescuers, but he was restrained by the third who remained in the boat.

"Let them go to her," he said kindly. "You need to rest before you have a heart attack, too."

The rescued man sat opposite the women, holding his head in his hands, apparently unwilling to speak, or to be spoken to. It was nearly thirty minutes before the two men returned— alone. Ginny could tell from their faces that they bore only grim news, but the man was not aware of them until they began to climb into the boat.

He looked up startled and cried out, "Where is she?"

One man bowed his head while the other put his hand on the man's shoulder and said, "I'm really sorry, but she was already gone. There was nothing we could do. We'll take you to the shelter and send someone back for her."

"Oh, God, no," he sobbed. "She wanted to sit out the storm. She thought it would be a great experience to tell the grand-children. But she had no idea how bad it would be, and she was really scared. That's probably what killed her." He continued to sob quietly.

Ginny didn't know what to do or say. How do you comfort a complete stranger? What was running through her mind was how the couple had brought the tragedy on themselves when the truth struck her with stunning clarity that she and Melba were no different than this pathetic man. They'd deliberately chosen to put themselves in mortal jeopardy out of so-called concern for a dog. Did it ever occur to her for a moment how it would affect Leland and Donald if she had died? They had behaved selfishly and irresponsibly. She could claim it was Melba's fault, but she knew better. She'd insisted that Melba come visit, and the whole chain of events had arisen because of her preoccupation with herself and her perceived unhappiness. How had she become so totally self-engrossed?

She looked at the sobbing man across from her and envisioned Leland sitting there, devastated over losing her.

She reached over spontaneously and took the man's hand. "I'm so sorry," she said, "so very, very sorry." And it was much more than the loss of his wife that she was referring to.

Thirty-One

The man at the wheel steered the boat slowly around the end of the building and headed east across the inland waterway toward the mainland. Ginny, looking south, could see the remains of the Stickney Point bridge. The middle section, which could be raised to let sailboats with tall masts through, had been torn loose and pieces lay at oblique angles against the piers. On the opposite shore, the storm surge had decimated the once-beautiful homes that had been built along the water's edge.

Their boat finally touched dry land a block east of where the shore had once been. The area was teeming with rescue vehicles and emergency medical personnel. The three of them were helped out of the boat and led over to an emergency squad van. Two young EMS technicians motioned them to sit on folding chairs that had been placed in haphazard rows in the middle of a front yard.

"We want to make sure you are physically okay before we take you to a shelter," said one who began wrapping a blood pressure cuff around Ginny's arm. The other one, a woman, was doing the same thing to Melba.

"Are you feeling okay? Any complaints?"

He placed the stethoscope on her arm and pumped up the cuff before she could answer. "A little high, but not dangerously so," he said taking off the cuff.

"After what I've been through I'm surprised it's not through the roof," Ginny said. "And I'm feeling fine now that I'm on dry land."

He put his fingers gently on her wrist. "Uh-huh. Your pulse is a little fast, too."

"Of course it is. I'm real anxious to get over to Phillipi School so I can find my husband."

He smiled at her. What a pleasant young man. "I don't see any reason you shouldn't go."

She looked over toward Melba and saw that she wasn't quite finished. She opened her purse and took out her compact, comb and lipstick. She hadn't had time even to comb her hair before they left.

Her reflection in the mirror shocked her. She couldn't believe two days could affect her appearance so markedly, but she looked awful. Her hair was a matted mess; she realized she hadn't even run a comb through it since before the storm, and she wore no makeup. But that could all be rectified. What concerned her was the fact she had visibly aged—the pouches under her eyes were more pronounced, the wrinkles seemed deeper. She felt like Dorian Gray who had been exempted from the aging process by a portrait that took on all the manifestations of old age in his place. And then one awful day, all the ravages of time were transferred from the picture onto his still-youthful face, turning him into a hideous old man.

Obviously, the change on her couldn't compare to Dorian Gray's metamorphosis, but she was certain the past two days had left an indelible imprint on her face.

Melba was finished now and walked over to her sister. "They want me to go to the hospital and get checked over. It seems my blood pressure's sky high."

Ginny was alarmed. "I'm going with you."

"No, I'll be fine, really. With all that's happened I forgot to take my medication, that's all. I insist you go on over to the school so you can find Leland. Then if you want, you can come and visit me."

"Are you sure?"

"Cross my heart." She smiled and made a big X over her heart the way they had always done when they were kids.

"Okay, then, but if you need me, you have them get hold of me at the school, and I'll be right over."

Melba seemed very calm now. If she had acted the least upset, Ginny would have insisted on going with her, but her sister wouldn't hear of it. So she kissed Melba on the cheek. "Take care, then, and we'll be over as soon as I can track Leland down."

The technician led Melba to the passenger seat of the EMS van and they drove away toward the hospital which was just a few blocks north off of Osprey Avenue. The man who'd been rescued with them was still being checked over by medical personnel. Although he was silent, his grief was so tangible it was almost contagious, and Ginny was anxious to leave. She'd barely held it all together for so long she was afraid of coming completely unglued if she was around him too much longer, so she was relieved when a volunteer driver asked if she wanted to go to the school.

He let her out at the front entrance to Phillipi School. Children were playing on the swings and monkey bars as if nothing out of the ordinary had happened. The sound of children laughing and shouting seemed to Ginny the most positive sign yet. Life does go on, even after the worst of disasters.

Inside, the gym was teeming with people milling around, sitting on folding chairs, lying on mattresses on the floor. The Red Cross had set up a table across the back of the gym to serve food, and a long line had queued up around the north wall waiting to get breakfast. She went to the end of the food line and leaned wearily against the tile wall as the queue inched its way toward the table. She was staring blankly at the markings on the gym floor beneath her feet, concentrating on the worn white lines the way a subject being hypnotized would stare at a swinging watch, when she heard someone call out her name.

She looked up and saw Nicholas coming toward her, a look of joy on his face. He encircled her with a bear hug, locking her in an embrace as though she belonged to him. At first she panicked, worried about such an open display of affection from him, but then she felt foolish. Who was paying any attention to them anyway? Everyone there was wrapped up in his or her own concerns; no one cared in the slightest what they were doing.

He finally let go and held her at arms' length. "Thank God you're okay. I was afraid I wouldn't be able to find you. Where's Melba?"

"Her blood pressure was high so they took her to the hospital to keep an eye on her. I'll be going over to see her as soon as I can find Leland."

"He's not back yet?"

"I don't know. We just got off Siesta Key a little while ago. They had to rescue us by boat. I imagine he's on his way by now, but I don't know when they were able to leave Islamorada."

"Ginny," he was all solemnity now, "can we go outside where we can talk privately?"

This was not the time for serious discussions—she could only imagine what he wanted to say—but she didn't know how to refuse him, either.

He guided her out a side door away from the playground area where it was relatively quiet, the children's voices muted now on the far side of the building. There was a low stone wall, and he motioned for her to sit on it.

"I've been frantic with worry over you," he said. "I had visions of your condo collapsing, or of you trying to reach dry land and being swept away by the storm surge. You've no idea what I've been through." His normally placid face was crimped into a frown that was utterly foreign to him.

She couldn't help but smile a little. "What you've been through? It couldn't compare to what we've been through."

"Do you want to talk about it?"

"Not now. Maybe later. I'm still numb."

"You're still in shock. But when you're ready to talk, I'm always available to listen. What I really want to discuss, though, is us."

He looked at her expectantly, waiting for her to respond.

"I'm not ready to talk about that either."

"Okay, I understand. I do have to say one thing though. This experience made me realize more than ever how important you are to me. I don't know what I'd have done if anything had happened to you, Ginny. And I had to let you know that."

She was trying desperately to feel something, to respond, if only internally, to his concern and love. But she couldn't. Only a void seemed to exist where her emotions should have been. She felt like a damned automaton. Did disasters short-circuit your feelings? Did everything become numb to protect you from overload?

She began to cry. Nicholas gathered her in his arms again to comfort her and she didn't resist. But the strange thing was she was crying not from overwhelming emotions, but for lack of them. This emptiness was the most terrible reaction of all.

She felt better when the tears stopped and pulled away from Nicholas. "I think you'd better not be around when Leland gets back. Why don't you go see how Melba is doing? I'm worried about her."

"Are you certain you're okay?"

"Oh, sure. Just worn out."

"Why don't you go lie down in the gym while you're waiting?"

"I will, Nicholas. I've managed to take care of myself pretty well so far." She knew she sounded cross, but sometimes his solicitousness got on her nerves.

Finally convinced that she really wanted him to go, he left for the hospital, but only after she promised to think about their future while she was waiting for Leland. She assured him she would, although she knew she had neither the energy nor desire to consider it now.

She went back to the food line and realized that while her emotions might be in limbo, her appetite certainly was not. She wished the line would move a lot faster. The smell of coffee brewing was so tantalizing she could hardly bear to wait. After half an hour of inching her way slowly forward, she selected a couple of doughnuts, orange juice, and coffee and looked around for somewhere to sit and eat. Every available space was taken so she went out the door on the playground side of the building, and miraculously, found an empty swing. She perched on it, the doughnuts in her lap, the orange juice and coffee on the ground beside her.

The other swings were all occupied by exuberant children, and she could feel the pulse of their energetic pumping coursing down the chains of her swing, sending their rhythms through her body. It was almost as if their energy was flowing into her. Oh, children, she thought, how you reaffirm the joy of life with your immutable liveliness. How can anyone feel down when there is the laughter of children to lift you up?

The sky was completely clear now, and it was hard to believe that the past two days had actually happened. It was just another warm, sunny day in Sarasota, Florida, and although it seemed a little incongruous to be sitting on a swing on a school playground, she'd always felt at home with children, whether at the beach making sand castles or sharing their swing set.

A police car pulled up to the curb as she was drinking her coffee. A man stepped out, his back to her, and turned to speak to the driver, his head ducked down to the level of the car's roof. But the chino pants and plaid shirt were familiar, and the gray curls, only barely visible from her position on the swing, were unmistakable. Before he straightened up and turned around she knew it was Leland. She leaped from the swing and ran toward him, unaware that her cup of coffee had slipped from her hand and the doughnuts were flung to the ground.

Such an overwhelming sense of gladness took hold of her, so unexpectedly, that she was shaken by it. She'd been consumed by hurt and resentment for so long that she'd forgotten how such an emotion could flow through her entire being, causing her to imagine she could almost levitate, in spirit if not in body. She could barely sense the ground under her feet. If her feelings had been short-circuited for the past several days, they were now exquisitely acute.

He had turned around and was looking over the playground area but had not yet seen her.

"Leland, I'm here!" she called as she detoured around a seesaw. The din from the children almost drowned out her voice, but he seemed to have heard it and turned in her direction.

"Ginny!" He saw her now and his face changed instantaneously from a worried frown to a look of unmistakable relief.

Their embrace was prolonged and intense, totally different from the pecks on the cheek that had recently served as affection. Ginny didn't want to let go. She hadn't realized until this minute how desperately she missed him during her ordeal. She knew she'd performed well during the hurricane; she had surprised even herself. But the numbness that had overcome her had masked her need for him, for his *being there*. He was a part of her, an important, life-confirming part.

"I've never been so glad to see you in my life," she said as they clung to each other.

"Oh, Ginny, me too." He stepped back and put his hands on her shoulders, looking her over. "Thank God, you're okay. Where's Melba?"

"They're keeping an eye on her in the hospital. Her blood pressure's up because she didn't take her pills."

"She forgot them when you came to the shelter?"

She took his hand. "Come with me. We need to talk." She led him to the stone wall behind the school where she'd sat with Nicholas not an hour earlier.

"So tell me what happened," Leland said. "You'll never know how frantic I've been not knowing what's been going on."

"I've a confession to make."

"About what?" He was frowning now, and she steeled herself against the reaction she expected.

"I just got to the school a short while ago. We stayed at the condo . . ."

"But you promised!" He couldn't quite pull off his attempt to scold. There was too much concern in his voice.

"I know I did." She couldn't look him in the eye. Instead she traced with her forefinger the crack where two stones met on the top of the wall. They'd been shaped so that their curves fit together exactly. Finally she looked up at him. "I could say it was all Melba's fault, that she wouldn't leave without Mickey. But I should have insisted and dragged her out. My problem is I always shrink from controversy. I'd rather go along with things than have a confrontation."

Leland nodded. "Yes, and I tend to take advantage of it." He grinned slightly at his confession before resuming his serious expression as if he remembered he was supposed to be chastising her.

"Mickey is dead."

"What happened?" His eyes widened in apprehension.

"The picture window blew in. A piece of glass was imbedded in his neck and he bled to death."

"Oh, my God, Ginny, that could have been you!" His voice cracked with emotion.

"Our place is ruined, Leland. The window in the guest bedroom broke too, and the furniture's been destroyed. The storm surge went right through the lobby. The outside steps are gone from the middle of the second floor down. We had to be rescued by boat."

Leland stood up and pulled Ginny into his arms. She realized he was crying, something she hadn't seen since Donald had gotten into trouble years ago. "I'm so sorry. I'm so sorry," he murmured in her ear.

"You don't need to be sorry. It was my own stupidity."

He pulled away. "I'm so sorry for being such a jerk these past months. I had a lot of time to think on Islamorada, and I realized I'd given you pretty short shrift while I indulged in my hobbies. It occurred to me I'd been frantically keeping busy so I wouldn't have to stop and assess my life. I was afraid of what I'd find. Or not find."

"Like what?"

"Like my identity. Who I am now that I'm not Mr. Development Manager any more."

Ginny shook her head in wonder. "I guess that's what we've both been doing. Don't you think we'd know who we are at our age?"

"Maybe that's something you have to work out over and over in your life." Leland stroked her arm as if wanting to make sure she was really there.

"Maybe so." She agreed.

"Well, why don't we try to work on it together instead of separately."

"Sounds good to me."

"I know how we can start." Leland said.

"How?"

"Let's get off that island. It's too dangerous to live there. Let's take whatever insurance money we get and look for another place. Where do you want to live, Ginny? Do you want to stay here? Go back to Columbus?"

That caught her off guard. "You'd really do that, Leland? Live in Columbus for my sake?"

He looked at her very seriously. "I want more than anything else for you to be happy, Ginny."

She fingered the collar of his shirt thoughtfully and then reached up and stroked his cheek. "I know how much you love it here. I feel sure if we lived in a neighborhood of mixed ages I'd be content. Besides I'm beginning to find my niche here."

He caught her up in a bear hug that almost took her breath away. "That's right, you are. Have you ever thought that this whole experience might be the basis for one heck of a poem?"

"A poem?" laughed Ginny. "I thought you considered writing poetry a waste of time."

Leland looked shame-faced. "I guess it's no more a waste of time than golf or fishing. I can't expect you to understand my needs if I don't understand yours."

"Well, we're not always going to agree on everything, darling. But I think we've both learned how important it is to keep an open mind."

Ginny knew she had to see Nicholas one last time to tell him her answer was no. She hoped he wouldn't have too much trouble dealing with it. And she probably would never go back to the poetry group; it would be too awkward with Nicholas there.

But she would find other groups that she could connect with and other interests as well. The storm had done more than take away her home; it had erased her doubts and fears about where her life was headed now. It was headed into one of those glorious sunsets with Leland, the one true love of her life.

ABOUT THE AUTHOR

Nancy Gotter Gates is the author of four mysteries, one set in Sarasota, Florida and three set in Greensboro, North Carolina. She has also published twenty-nine short stories as well as dozens of poems and articles. She lives in a retirement community in High Point, North Carolina with her cat Annie.